THE MILKMAN'S ON HIS WAY

We were announced as the winners by Hughie
Green – the audience applauded loudly and long,
we stood there awkwardly basking in the adulation.

'What will it be this week, boys?' asked Hughie
Green.

'We have written a song, it's called, "You Only
Have To Smile",' said Jim.

'Who wrote the words and who wrote the
music?'

'He wrote the words and the music,' I said, pointing at Jim.

'But he just said a song we had written – where
do *you* come in?'

'I lent him the pencil,' I said.

Also by Max Bygraves in *Star*

I WANNA TELL YOU A STORY

THE MILKMAN'S ON HIS WAY

Max Bygraves

A STAR BOOK

published by
the Paperback Division of
W. H. ALLEN & Co. Ltd

A Star Book
Published in 1978
by the Paperback Division of W. H. Allen & Co. Ltd.
A Howard and Wyndham Company
44 Hill Street, London W1X 8LB

First published in Great Britain by
W. H. Allen & Co. Ltd, 1977

Printed in Great Britain by
Richard Clay (The Chaucer Press), Ltd., Bungay, Suffolk

ISBN 0 352 30170 8

First of all, get this straight – I didn't want to be a milk-man. I'd have done anything: brain surgeon, police super-intendent – anything – it was just that when I walked into this Labour Exchange in Battersea, the poof behind the counter said: 'Fancy a milkman?' I said: 'Don't be a clot!' I'm like that with words – if he had said: 'Fancy a baker?' I'd have had a comeback like: 'Yes – I'm rather well-bred.' But as I said, he held this card up and said: 'Go on, blue eyes – have a go at a milkman.' I said: 'I'll have a go at you!' He threw his eyes up towards the fluorescent ceiling and lisped: 'Promises, promises!'

'All right, bung it over,' I said. I had been going there for eight weeks – I had to show willing. It was wrong to keep collecting my dole and not show willing, they were getting a bit fed up with me at the exchange. A few days before, I had been sent to Harrods' dispatch department – it was lunchtime when I got there, they were out at lunch, I went into the store to browse – finished up buying a shirt and tie to match – came to nine quid – I was so eager to get home and try them on I forgot all about the card I had to produce at the dispatch department. When I got back to the flat it fell out of my pocket. I wrote 'unsuitable' on it.

Next day, I took it back to the clerk: 'Why were you unsuitable for Harrods?' he asked. ''Cos me name is Self-ridge, ain't it!'

It's a fact too, my name is Harry Selfridge – twenty-two years of age, Battersea born and bred, one surviving relative – mother, who drinks a bit – just coming up for fifty and not averse to 'having it off'.

I stand almost six feet – another three quarters of an inch would do it – but I'm not bothered. I've got these Cuban heels that stack me another two inches, they look good but they're bloody uncomfortable to wear. I've got blond hair, well sort of blond, now and again I get a brush and put a bit of the old lady's peroxide on to 'streak' it. Sometimes I treat myself to a bottle of that suntan stuff that makes you look like a Rhodesian – you've got to be careful with that though, because you've got to get it on even, otherwise you look as if somebody has thrown a handful of horse-shit at you through a chain-link fence.

I took the card, which was for a milk roundsman at Dutton's Dairies, not too far from our high riser that overlooks the Thames, and had to walk round to the address.

I ambled into the yard that was scattered with little electric carts carrying crates of empty bottles, there was a lot of whistling going on amongst the fellows who had finished their rounds. I made a mental note that this was 'a happy ship'.

'Where's the gaffer?' I asked one of the roundsmen, who looked as if he had been a milkman all his life – he was the same shape as a pint of gold top. He jerked his thumb towards a sign that said 'Office'.

'In there, ain't it?' I hate those bloody fellows that answer a question with a question.

'Is it?' I said.

'Well, it always was, wasn't it?' he said.

'Was it?' I said.

He looked at me for the first time: 'What d'ya want?'

I said: 'Have you got two raspberry yoghurts?'

He said: 'You taking the piss?'

I said: 'Yes please – two pints!'

He said: 'Piss off!' So I did.

The office had three desks in it – at one was some old dear with glasses right on the tip of her nose, she kept pushing a calculator that kept vomiting paper with little black figures on, she had a fag lit with an inch of ash on. I kept expecting it to fall as she coughed but it stayed there, she coughed each time she pressed the machine – the cigarette was now almost burning the filter at the end, she reached out for a saucer that was filled with about twenty other dog-ends, let it drop into the ashes and without taking her eyes off the list in front of her, lit a new cigarette – as she took a fresh puff, she gave another three coughs. She was the perfect advertisement for lung cancer.

The other desk was occupied by another woman much younger – she was pounding a typewriter, now and again she'd stop to drink from a mug of black coffee with a picture of Winston Churchill on it.

I guess she must have been in her early forties and was attractive in a funny sort of way – her hair was black and piled high with one twist that made it look very much like a beehive. I had the feeling that if I pulled the large Spanish comb from it, a swarm of bees would have emerged and buzzed round the office.

The last one was a little darling – honey-coloured hair, big eyes, an hour-glass figure with all the sand at the top, she was sucking a ball-point pen that she took from her mouth now and then to note something.

None of them looked up when I entered the office. I let about half a minute tick by, then interrupted the proceedings by saying: 'Excuse me, can you tell me where you keep the goat, I have to get some fresh milk.'

Everything stopped and the office became still. Miss Woodbine, the old dear with cigarette and cough, said: 'Goat?'

'I'm only kidding.' It went over like a lead balloon. 'I've come for a job as a milkman.'

'Oh,' said Old Smokey, 'have you got a card?'

I handed her the card the employment exchange had

7

given me – she looked down her glasses and read aloud: 'Harry Selfridge.' She looked over the top of her spectacles again: 'Have you ever done anything like it before?'

'I worked for a brewery once.'

'H'mm, I don't think that's anything like a milk rounds-man.'

'I used to deliver the milk stout.' I fluttered my eyes.

It was a waste of time, I wasn't going to get any laughs from this trio, so I got right on with it. 'Will you mark it "unsuitable" and I'll get out of your way.' I didn't want to hang around too long because there was a Steve McQueen film at the Odeon and I didn't want to miss the afternoon performance. I had promised a couple of the lads I would see them in the Tavern for a game of darts and a drink at seven.

'How do I know you're unsuitable – it's up to the boss,' said the cough drop.

'Where is he?'

'Wait there,' she said. She left the office and I could feel the young one eyeing me. I winked at her, she dropped her head and went back to her notes. I looked out of the window onto the yard. The men were putting bottles into large containers that were then going through a washing process. I turned round to see the young one studying me – I put my tongue out and slowly brought it across my lips, she gave a half smile and dropped her head again. I thought to myself: 'Harry, if you had been working here, you could have had that in a few days.'

The door to another office opened and in came Miss Fumes – there was a cracker of about twenty with her, dressed in a pink two-piece, breasts high, good legs in comfortable shoes and a smile that played around the corners of her mouth. 'Mr Selfridge?' she asked. I nodded.

'Do you want to work for Dutton's?'

She was gorgeous. Even white teeth, lipstick that was

8

almost the same colour as the two-piece she was wearing, a trace of eye shadow and a skin that bloomed. I thought: 'What an advert for milk – I'll start tomorrow.' I nodded again to her question.

'When can you start?'

'Any time,' I stammered.

Her eyes held me, they were lovely, I forgot I was a lay-about, suddenly I wanted to work for this vision.

'Could you begin tomorrow?'

'Yes, madam.'

'Well, we start early in the milk business, can you be here by five a.m.?'

I thought: 'Go easy – that's the time I usually *go* to bed – not get up.'

'Yes, madam,' I stammered again.

She then proceeded to tell me that I would start with one of the regular milkmen who would show me the round, load the truck, make the books up, collect payment – count the eggs, butter, yoghurts, etc., then in two weeks I would have my own round.

I would have to be there just after five a.m. I would expect to finish around midday, there was all weekend off, I would get a commission and would average forty pounds a week. She signed my card D. E. Dutton. I took it back to the exchange, they said they would send my stamp cards on.

What was wrong with me, what possessed me to look into the eyes of a girl and agree to become a milkman? I had always prided myself on the way I lived on the State, now here I was agreeing to work! Work! The very thought made me shudder. As I walked from the exchange to the flat, a cat was walking in front of me. It occurred to me that I might be going soft, so I kicked it up the arse.

When I got home, the 'old lady' was there with Mr Benson.

9

She worked at the school a couple of streets away cooking school dinners. Mr Benson was the school caretaker, his visits had been getting more regular, he always wore a collar and tie with his dungarees. He sucked a pipe with a tobacco brand that was advertised on television. When they did the advert on TV it showed a guy in a peak cap putting a match to his pipe and lighting the very same tobacco that 'Benjy' smoked, immediately the violins on the soundtrack cascaded and dozens of female heads jerked towards the model with the pipe. When Benjy lit his, it seemed as if the power station down the road from us had suddenly lit all four chimneys, it smelt like he had set light to a compost heap. We lived on the ninth floor of the flats but I always knew when he was there, I could smell him as I got in the lift.

'Hello Harry boy,' he said. 'Where've you been – snooker?'

'No, I've been after a job.' I tried to act nonchalant.

There was stone silence.

'A job?' said the old lady. 'A job with money?' I nodded.

'Where?' asked Benjy – this was my secret name for him. I always called him Mr Benson to his face. He had been caretaker at the school I went to and we were always taught to refer to him as Mister, it seemed strange to hear the old lady call him 'Vic'. Whenever she said Vic to him, I always thought of that stuff she used to rub my chest with.

'At Dutton's Dairies,' I sighed.

'When?'

'Tomorrow.'

'What time?'

'I'll have to be up at four.'

'Up at four!'

'Who's going to call you?'

'I'll put the alarm on.'

'It don't work – you'll never be up!' she said.

'Don't worry, I'll get up.'

'You get up,' she said. 'Hark at Rip Van Winkle – you can't even get up in time to watch Coronation Street.'

They both laughed loudly at this. I suddenly felt a great urge to push the pipe into Benjy's mouth and block his windpipe, but I let it pass.

'I'll ask the Dempseys to lend me theirs,' I said.

The Dempseys lived next door – Johnny the eldest son worked over at Smithfield meat market and had to be in at seven, I had often heard their alarm clock go off when I was trying to get to sleep after a night out with the lads.

'Are you serious?' asked the old lady.

'He'll stick it for a couple of days,' said Benjy knowingly.

'He's raving mad,' said the old lady.

I walked into my bedroom and lay on the bed, I gazed at the ceiling and began thinking.

I thought, here am I twenty-two years of age, at a dead end. The farthest I ever travelled was to the Isle of Wight to see a pop festival three years ago. I hadn't even been to Spain on a package holiday, all my mates had been, they talked about their exploits on the Costa da Fortune, chatting up Spanish birds, while all I could talk about was the Isle of Wight ferry.

I had never kept a job more than a week, except at a florists where I had managed to hold one for ten weeks. It was all right delivering those wedding bouquets and anniversary bunches of carnations, they always came to the door smiling, but those funerals were a drag. They answered my knock red-eyed, and gaunt faced – I got to dread it. See, I like to laugh, I like making up jokes – I'm no Morecambe and Wise but now and again I do come up with a funny one, you know, one that I'm really proud of, like the time I was working for the builder's merchants – I had mucked an order up, the boss got on the blower to tear me off a strip, one of the carpenters said: 'Harry, the boss is on the 'phone!' I said: 'That must be uncomfortable.' I got the sack but it made the others laugh.

From this you must deduce that I wasn't really the one to deliver wreaths to the bereaved, but I liked the job, I had my own little van that I borrowed at weekends, I wasn't supposed to but I had two sets of keys. As I say, I was only there for ten weeks and I didn't much care – I had tried nearly a dozen jobs but out of all of them I kept thinking back to that florists, then, as I was thinking of the carnations and roses and daffodils and asters, Miss Dutton's face appeared amongst them, I also noticed I was getting on heat. I made up my mind to give the Tavern a miss and go to bed early so I could be at the milk depot for five a.m.

I borrowed the alarm clock from Johnny Dempsey and promised to leave it outside their door when I went off. That evening, when the old lady and Benjy were watching TV, I said goodnight and went to bed. I sat looking out of the window for a while, across the river at Chelsea. I suddenly found myself asking why people in those gorgeous houses and flats opposite spent thousands and thousands for leaseholds. Here was I, gazing at their lovely homes from a high riser in Battersea for a few quid a week and they were paying all that money to look at the piss-hole we lived in.

I put my jeans and leather top out with some woollen socks and wellingtons for the morning and went to sleep.

2

It seemed like just five minutes later that I woke to the clanging of the alarm. Christ, it was loud! I jumped out of bed and switched on the light. As I put my jeans on, I found myself thinking of my father. His trousers were like drainpipes, he had left home when I was ten but I can remember his Teddy-boy suit that he hung up carefully each time he'd finished wearing it, the highly polished winklepicker shoes, and bloody Brylcreem everywhere, he wasn't happy until that quiff he had in the front of his hair was like patent leather, and that bloody Brylcreem dripped from it. I wondered why I was thinking of somebody I hadn't seen for years at this hour and got on with combing my hair. This long hair might be fashionable but that too is a bloody drag, pity somebody didn't bring back short back and sides again, like the old fellows have.

I walked into the kitchen, there was half a pint of milk left in a bottle which I drank, the old lady would go mad when she found there wasn't any for her cup of tea, but sod her, she should have been up seeing a working man off.

I buttered two slices of bread and ate them, then I put my scarf on and walked out into the cold morning air, Jesus it was cold, I made a mental note to leave my pyjamas on under those jeans if it was going to be like this every morning. I still couldn't come up with an answer to why I was walking through the streets of Battersea with freezing balls, on my way to work at four-thirty a.m.

Dutton's was full of activity, the milk floats were being loaded by whistling men who stopped now and then to shout good morning to a new arrival. I stood watching them for a while, my teeth chattering with the cold, my hands dug deep in my jeans trying to keep my hands and my dick warm at the same time. I was just about to walk out of the gate and go home, back to bed, when a man in a brown warehouseman's coat said: 'You the new bloke?' I nodded. 'Right' he said, 'You go out with Jimmy Lloyd.'

'Where is he?' I asked.

'Over there.' He pointed to a cheerful man of forty-five or so, who was in the middle of the chorus of 'Delilah'.

'My my my Delilah ...' he warbled. 'Why why why Delilah ...'

'Jimmy Lloyd?' I asked.

'Right son – you the new bloke?'

I nodded again.

He right away gave me a run down on the job. He told me that his round was over the bridge in Chelsea, from Wandsworth Bridge down to Albert Bridge and took in most of those great big houses that had been converted into flats along the embankment. We'd make two journeys with a fully-loaded float that took us up to ten o'clock, we had an hour for breakfast at ten, then went back to the depot to check up, unload, get changed and go home. After he told me all this, he asked: 'All right Harry?' I liked him calling me by my Christian name. He smiled and went back to 'Delilah'. I helped to stack the crates of fresh milk onto the float. This made me feel a bit warmer.

When we were loaded, Jimmy opened a vacuum flask and poured some steaming tea from it, he punctured the metal top of a pint of pasteurised and added it to the tea. 'Get it down you,' he said pleasantly. 'It's the last you'll get for a few hours.' I drank it thankfully, he waited for me to finish, poured one out for himself, drank it,

14

then said: 'OK Harry — the wagons roll!' We sat in the front, he pressed the starter and we were on out way, crossing the Thames as Big Ben bashed out the hour of six.

I hadn't given much thought to a milkman before, it's bloody hard work, apart from the elements there's the weight of it all.

Milk is bloody heavy, when you get a pint into a thick glass bottle and then carry a couple of dozen of those up a few stairs several times, it's exhausting. You have to return with the empties, drive the cart, load the crate, get the empties, drive the cart, load the empties, look at the book, check who wants a jar of full cream, who wants butter, who wants eggs, it's bloody back-breaking work, on top of all this, you have a leather money bag draped round you, some people pay cash every time you deliver, they don't like to run up a bill, there are other sods who run up a bill and hate the sight of you when you knock for the money.

All this I learned on the first morning out with Jimmy Lloyd, I tagged behind him like a faithful dog, watching how he did it. There were a few insomniacs waiting for him to have a chat, he'd cheerfully talk with them, he talked about the weather, Chelsea's chances of getting in the Cup, television shows, the Government. He seemed to know instinctively what they wanted to chat about, I stood and watched him as a pupil watches a master, I admired him, I also wondered as I watched him whether I could ever be as good as he, he was so well liked too.

At most houses he just left the milk outside the door, retrieved the empty bottles and went 'Delilah-ing' on his way, so it became a fairly fast business. I couldn't believe it when he said 'Come on, let's have a bit of breakfast.' He drove to a café in a small street at the back of the King's Road, took about forty pints inside and sat at one of the

15

tables. A bleary-eyed Italian brought a large plate of fried eggs, tomatoes and toast, Jimmy said: 'Same for my mate.'

Five minutes later, I was eating the eggs and bacon while Jimmy studied the *Daily Mail*, he had finished his and lit a tiny cigar that had a nice aroma. Still reading his paper, without looking up he said: 'What d'ye think?'

'About what?'

'About being a milkman.'

'I dunno.'

'D'ye think you'll like it?'

'I can't say – I don't mind it up to now.'

'It's not too bad a morning now but some days it pisses down – then it's awful.'

'How long have you been a milkman?'

'Since I came out of the Navy.'

'Were you in the Navy?'

'Seven years.'

He knocked the ash off his little cigar and began to fold his paper which he put in his pocket. He continued.

'Been round the world half a dozen times.'

'How long you been a milkman?'

'Coming up for twenty years – it's the only job I could think of with no superiors hanging over you twenty-four hours a day – on board ship, you have everybody from a petty officer to the captain a few feet away from you, day after day, week after week – it's only when you go on leave you get away from them, they get a stripe, most of them, and they think it's their duty to make life as hard as they can for every rating aboard. I made up my mind when I got out there was going to be none of that, no factory chargehands, no guvnors, I'd do my work and do it properly, they could like it or lump it – nobody has complained so far – including me, I make a living, not a fortune but I'm practically my own boss.'

I said: 'Does the boss at Dutton's leave you alone?'

16

'She does.'

'She?' I said.

'Eileen Dutton is the boss, the old man died two years ago and young Eileen has been running it, she does a pretty good job too.'

My mind went back to the office yesterday – he must be talking about the one that took me on. I pumped Jimmy to tell me more about her, he went on to explain that the owner, John Dutton, had died suddenly leaving the entire company to his only child, she had left her studies to run the business and keep the staff in full employment. Most of that staff had been with Dutton's for many years, although she was fighting a battle with the large combines, she was managing to survive and keep everybody happy.

I suddenly got an overwhelming desire to look at her again – I can't explain it, after all, I don't go short of crumpet. I am not unattractive to birds, I can get most of them going and finish up in kip, I operate pretty well in those fields. I have a few that would like to go steady, but no – I mean I'm no Paul Newman but I'm not bad looking, they like my eyes, they keep getting on about my long lashes when I've got them in the pit. I've got one – Kathy Donnell – sometimes she says to me, 'Harry, just look at me.' This is in the middle of it all – the two of us stark naked, passions at fever pitch and she says that: 'Just look at me!' I think she's a bit kinky, I mean when a fellow's got a heat that feels like it's going to explode and there's a bird saying, 'Harry, look at me,' it's not normal, is it? But this Miss Dutton – Eileen – I wanted to see her again. We were poles apart, she had that, I suppose it's Roedean or wherever girls who are going to be ladies go – accent. I can't explain it so it's no use trying – I just wanted to see her, like a fellow who sees the Crown Jewels and wants to go a second time in the same day.

'It depends how you want it,' said Jimmy. 'If you like

freedom – you could do a lot worse – I don't think I can remember more than three days in twenty years when I've regretted it – but it takes all sorts to make a world.'

With this bit of philosophy, he drank his tea said, 'Cheerio!' to the Italian and departed with me running behind. I wondered who had paid for the breakfast, when I asked he said: 'Forget it – on the house.' We drove over the bridge again to get loaded up once more.

Eileen Dutton sat in the office of Dutton's Dairies. In front of her was a mass of correspondence, she pored over some of the problems that had been nagging her most – she asked herself what her father would have done but couldn't come up with an answer.

Her father had died two years ago, she had been at finishing school down in Sussex – the entire works had been left to her but with all the benefits had come the problems.

When she had inherited the dairy, she found at least half of the forty-four employees were past their mid-fifties. To have sold the business would have been an easy way out, but most of the people still working for Dutton's had been with her father since he began a small dairy back in the early thirties. Since then he had made a milk round into two milk rounds, then taken on another roundsman and then another. As he expanded, he found devoted workers and they were with the dairy till this day – a couple of them were nearing seventy, they refused to retire and Eileen was glad of them because labour was not easy to get these days. Most of the young men were going into the building trade where the money was far above what a milk roundsman could get, or else they went into factories and if the pay wasn't what they wanted, they could always strike.

It was imperative that workers at Dutton's did not strike

18

because unlike a factory that made cars or building materials, the dairy business couldn't stand it. Eggs, cheese and butter, apart from milk, cannot be kept like raw materials, they had to be delivered almost the same day. If she'd had strikes or disagreements too often, it could put her out of business, the small dairy could not stand the financial strain.

It was obvious she would have to give pay rises to nearly all, but where was it to come from? The government gave the word when to raise milk prices, you just couldn't say to the consumers that milk was going up a penny a pint, yet she had to come up with higher wages soon because loyalty is all right up to a degree but as her father had always told her, don't always go by the books, remember that human nature has a funny way of showing how it works with the most surprising results. Sometimes it is shown in kindness, tenderness, gentleness but it also shows itself in greed, bitterness and cheating. Her father had tried to tell her never to be surprised at it, allow for it and life is that little more tolerable.

She looked at the reams of paper she had to deal with. There were packets stamped OHMS, in them would be PAYE forms, tax deduction forms, accounts from the telephone exchange, forms to be filled in about milk handling, subsidy forms, forms for national insurance, forms for new employees, old employees, schedule D forms, fire prevention forms, hygiene forms and forms that told you how to fill up forms. There were insurance forms, road tax forms, vehicle insurance forms, forms, forms, forms, soon they became a blur, she lit a cigarette and gazed out of the window into the yard.

Just arrived in was Jim Lloyd with the new chap from the labour exchange. She wondered how long it would be before he would be knocking at the door asking for his cards. She had learned from her short experience that young fellows couldn't face the life, a milkman seems to be an easy way of life until you try it. Fellows who took on the job usually left in the first week, a few gave it a month or so, but in the last year she could only remember one who had persevered – Clarence Rodgers. Clarence was mad about nature study, the afternoons off appealed to him, he would go off to Wandsworth Common in summer and watch the butterflies or go down to Epping Forest in spring to talk to the squirrels. He was a good worker – most of those in the dairy considered him a joke but Eileen liked Clarence.

She watched Harry Selfridge unload and then reload the float out in the yard – it crossed her mind what an attractive man he was – slim, lithe, blond and blue-eyed, she noticed he had very long lashes.

I had been at the job for nearly a week now and I liked what I was doing. The early spring had come in as if it had been pressed from an atomiser. All along the route the almond blossom was out, birds were in full song and I had grown very close to Jimmy Lloyd.

One morning during the break at the café, he looked at me and said : 'You'll be getting your own round soon.'

I nodded. 'I expect so.'

'I should think they'll keep you on this one and move me onto one of the others.'

'Will you mind?'

'Mind? No, a change is as good as a rest.' He paused then said :

'I'll miss you, Harry – you've been good company, it's really a lonely life this milkman lark, it's been good to talk to somebody.'

'I'll miss you too, Jim.'

'Do you ever go out for a drink on Saturdays?'

'Sometimes – why?'

'Well,' he stopped to light one of those little cigars he seemed to like. 'Well – I go to a little club over where I live at Southwood – I'm a member – Saturdays I take the kids and the missus with me, we have a singalong. I play my guitar ...'

'I didn't know you played guitar.'

'Not like your bloody rock and rollers. I play it Spanish style.'

'How long have you been playing?'

'I learned in the Navy. We called in at Barcelona and I bought this guitar, four quid that's all it was – cost a lot more today – there was a fellow on the boat taught me a few chords and I kept it up – I take it up the club and give them a tune – what I was going to say is if you've got nothing to do and you feel like it on a Saturday, come and have a noggin.'

'Thanks, Jim,' I said. 'I might do that – when?'

'I go most Saturdays – want to make it this Saturday?'

'Yeah – all right.'

'Come to the house and we'll go from there – forty-seven Meadow Road, just behind Southwood station – okay?'

'Okay!'

He seemed pleased. 'You'll enjoy it.' We drank our tea and got on with the round.

3

For some reason it felt good to be alive. I found myself singing a happy little tune, whistling as I went up and down stairs. One of the customers said to me on this particular day: 'I always know when you're coming milk-man – you always sound so happy.' I winked and said: 'It's being so cheerful that keeps me going.' Jim often said that – I think it was somebody's catchphrase on a radio programme during the war.

Another customer said to me: 'Do you have to be so bleedin' happy?' I said: 'No, mate, I could be like you and get a job sucking lemons.' That shut him up. There are some people around who, if they had their way, would stop the birds singing.

On Saturday afternoon, I got a shampoo, got my hair blown and went back home to put my suit on. The old lady was there with Benjy watching a TV film starring Betty Grable and Dan Dailey. Neither of them looked up as I walked in – I watched for about five minutes, then she glanced my way.

'What you all ponced up for?'

'I'm taking Elizabeth Taylor out tonight.'

'Oh – I hope you enjoy it.' She went back to the TV screen.

I had only one suit but it was a good one, what they call a Chester Barrie, it had cost me sixty quid, it was a con-servative dark blue pin-stripe. I knew I looked good in it – I got my pale blue shirt out and decided on my white tie; I put a big knot in the tie, buttoned the waistcoat, rubbed my shoes up and down the backs of my trouser legs, put what was left of my wages – twelve quid – in my pocket, and walked into the living-room.

'Ooh, look,' said the old lady, 'Here's Hardy Amies.'

Benjy said, 'Give my regards to Richard Burton.'

Under my breath, I said: 'Get stuffed.' Then left for Jim Lloyd's over at Southwood.

Jim lived in a semi-detached house in a tree-lined street named Meadow Road. Forty-seven was the nicest looking house in the entire road. It had a small garden with a solitary tree, which I think was a cherry tree, it was full of blossom and made the new cream paintwork on the windows and doors come to life. The mellow red brick of the house had a happy feel about it even from the out-side.

A ten- or eleven-year-old girl with blonde hair in plaits answered my knock. 'Hello – are you Mr Selfridge?' I nodded. 'Come in,' she said with a shy smile. I walked into a light hallway and on the small hall-table was a fading wedding photograph with Jim in sailor's uniform. The whole place had a clean fresh smell – in the distance I could hear laughter.

The girl showed me into the living-room and through two doors that opened to a back garden, I could see Jim lying full length on the grass being pounded by two young fair-haired boys of six or seven, they were twins, he had told me about them at different times on the round.

'Daddy,' shouted the little girl above the din. 'Daddy – Mr Selfridge is here!'

'Hello, Harry!' shouted Jim. 'That's enough lads – half time.' He got up with his hand extended, 'Come in, mate.'

The twins looked at me with curiosity, Jim brushed himself down saying at the same time: 'This is Timothy, this is Andrew and this one is Sheila.' I said 'Hello,' to them and Jim put his arm round my shoulder. 'Fancy a

23

cup of tea?' Without waiting for my reply, he said to
Sheila: 'Cup of tea for two, please miss.' The little girl
went inside to do as he bid.

'The wife's gone up the shops – she won't be long – sit
down mate – make yourself at home.' I sat down, the
twins sat at the other side of the room on a settee, just
gazing at me.

'I've just been checking the pools,' said Jimmy.

'Any luck?' I said.

'No – that flippin' Chelsea does it on me every week –
they play badly, I put them down to lose, they go away to
Leeds and then win – how can you bet on form like that?'

'Yes, they're not doing too well this year.'

'Not doing too well – I'll tell you Harry – Billy Graham
couldn't save them.'

Sheila came in with a small tray with a small china
teapot, two cups and saucers and some assorted biscuits.
'Have these till the wife gets home, then we'll have some
proper nosh,' he said.

The kids asked if they could watch some TV. We drank
our tea and munched biscuits, we made idle chatter for
about fifteen minutes. There was a loud rat-tat at the
door, one of the kids got up and opened it.

Into the room walked Mrs Lloyd – Daphne – she was
in her mid-forties, blonde like the kids, with a broad smile
that never seemed to leave her face.

'This is my trouble and strife, Daphne,' said Jim, he
got up and took the two big shopping bags she was carrying – they were filled with groceries and vegetables from
the greengrocers.

'Hello, Harry – I've heard a lot about you from Jim.' She
had a Midlands accent, I found out later she came from
Wolverhampton. We shook hands and she wandered into
the kitchen to unload – the kids were silent, watching
Dr Who. I watched with them and in another half hour we

24

were all sitting round the table eating a ham salad with pears and cream to follow.

After tea, there was a dispersal to bedrooms and bathrooms to get ready to go the the club. Jim had a Prince of Wales check suit on, Daphne had a plain navy dress with some pearls around her neck, the twins had freshly laundered shirts with flared long trousers and young Sheila wore jeans that matched top and bottom. At seven-thirty sharp we left for Jim's club, with both twins arguing who was going to carry Jim's guitar – to settle the argument, he told them they could carry it half way each. This pleased them. Timothy took it and Andrew walked behind, making sure he would not take it one step farther than what had been agreed was the halfway, the lamp-post at the end of Meadow Road.

The Southwood Social Centre was a fairly new all-purpose hall built on the side of a comprehensive school. Round the walls were rungs that were used by gymnasts, there were tables spaced out to face a small stage about two feet high.

On the stage was a piano and drum kit. As the hall filled up with families of all ages – from old ladies to babes in arms – two middle-aged fellas sat down at the piano and drums and began playing without any announcement or preamble. Several couples got up and danced.

There was a bar where two ladies in flowered overalls dispensed canned beer, lemonade, Coca Cola, meat pies, crisps, sandwiches – Jim got a dozen cans of light ale, some crisps and chocolate biscuits for the kids. He poured out a light ale for Daphne, one for me and one with an enormous white frothy head for himself – we all said, 'Cheers!' and settled down for a social evening.

Everybody knew Jim, they kept wandering over, slapping his back, shaking his hand, giving Daphne and the kids kisses and having laughs at the chatter between themselves. After about an hour there was a drum roll from the drummer, he stood up and announced that we would be entertained by the Great Spero, master magician.

The Great Spero turned out to be a Cockney conjurer who made handkerchiefs disappear, did some paper tearing and then invited two members of the audience to come up and help him with some card tricks. He was no David Nixon but he had a good line of patter, he was obviously used to this type of audience, he was inoffensive, clean with his jokes and had an answer for most of the barracking that was going on.

His last trick was to ask any lady in the audience to volunteer to be sawn in half. 'Here you are,' shouted Jim, 'take my old woman.' Daphne laughed as much as the audience and went along with the joke.

The Great Spero put her into a long coffin-like box with her feet sticking out of the bottom – all this was causing great merriment, the twins were having a big laugh too until they happened to see a big saw that Spero produced – suddenly their faces became serious and their fingers went to their mouths. Spero asked for another volunteer to help with the sawing and Jim got up to help, everybody was laughing heartily.

'Which half would you like?' Spero asked Jim. He came back with: 'I don't want the half that eats.'

They began to saw and we watched it go right through Daphne's middle. There was great applause as Spero produced her in one piece and walked her back to our table – the twins were relieved and rushed round to cuddle her. Andrew kept searching for the line he was sure would have been left by the saw. Sheila told him not to be daft and he went back to his coke, fully convinced that she would fall in half before the night was out.

The drummer announced that it was time for ... 'Our

very own Segovia to entertain.' To loud applause Jim got his guitar and walked up on the stage – the microphone was lowered, a chair was produced, the hall went very quiet and Jim began to play. It was quite a shock, he was brilliant, his fingers ran up and down the fretboard of the guitar, he picked at the strings and from it came a sound so beautiful it had all the flavour of, although I have never been there, Spain.

The melody was filled with romance and every person in the room was spellbound, even the small babies had stopped crying. As the last notes died away, the applause broke out, over the applause different people were calling for requests: 'South of the Border!' 'Marie Elena!' 'Delilah, Jim!' He obliged with several numbers and to a great reception he returned to our table and drank a whole light ale down in three gulps.

'Great, darling,' said Daphne.

'Great, dad,' said the kids.

Various people came over and shook Jim's hand. 'You get better.' 'Marvellous, Jim!' 'I could listen to you all night,' were some of the remarks.

When they had wandered off and we were alone, I said: 'I didn't know you played as well as that Jim lad.' He smiled.

'Why don't you do it professionally?' I asked. He was pleased with this but in his modest way he replied: ' 'Cos I'm not good enough.'

Jim said his goodnights at around ten-thirty, then picked up the twins and we all left for Meadow Road. Daphne said that if I didn't want to rush for the last bus, I could kip on the settee which she would make up. The family seemed to like me and I liked them, it was one of the best Saturday evenings I had spent for a long time. Sheila was drooping as we walked, so I picked her up and piggybacked her. Daphne was carrying Jim's guitar, Jim had the twins on either arm – as we walked, we all sang, 'I love to go a-wandering ...' As we Happy Wanderers reached the gate, the three kids were asleep.

We put them in their bedrooms, Daphne undressed them and Jim went into the kitchen to make a pot of tea. When we were all settled, Jim picked up his guitar, took it out of its case and began to strum. 'What's your favourite song, Harry?' I told him it was 'Blue Spanish Eyes'. 'I'm not sure of that – sing a bit of it.' I sang quietly: 'Blue Spanish Eyes ... teardrops are falling from those Spanish Eyes ...' Daphne had walked back into the room, I looked up. 'Don't stop, Harry, you've got a nice voice.'

I blushed up but she insisted: 'Go on – there's only us here.' I sang some more, I had never been told I had a voice before, I had joined in a few shout-ups before closing time trying to outdo the amplified guitars they had at the Tavern at weekends, but singing softly to Jim's guitar was a new experience. He seemed to cushion me, as I sang he made my notes much more tuneful.

'You've got a good range,' said Jim.

'It's a most unusual voice,' said Daphne, 'I like it.'

Jim played me some songs he had written and I thought that most of them were worthy of exploitation. I asked him if he ever played them at the club, he said that now and again he did but he didn't have a lot of confidence in them. One, a piece called, 'You only have to smile,' was a beautiful composition – he played it, I asked him to play it again and then again. By the third time I almost had it.

'Hey,' he said – 'It sounds great when you sing it quietly like that.'

As Daphne cleared up the crockery, she said, 'You two will be on *Opportunity Knocks* next.' We laughed – Jim had a last small cigar, Daphne made a bed up on the settee, I slipped my slacks undone but kept them on, covered myself and after I had put the light out started thinking how nice having a family can be.

I had never experienced anything like this – when my dad was at home and I was small, it was always baby-sitters, usually girls that would bung me off to bed as soon as my folks went out, then when they thought I was asleep they'd creep to the door and let a boyfriend in. I can remember when I was about seven, a baby-sitter and her bloke having it off in front of me. When I asked him what he was doing on top of the girl, he said: 'Riding a bike.'

I turned over and went to sleep quietly humming, 'You only have to smile'. I hoped that I would get to know Jim better, he was a great guy. I was going to enjoy being a milkman.

4

Eileen Dutton thought it best for me to take over Jim's round. Jim didn't mind, he went a little further afield, more towards the Wimbledon district but we'd meet in the yard, have a cup of tea and a chat. When it was time to finish, we usually strolled up to the Star to have a pint of bitter – we'd talk mostly about his songs, he wrote a new one almost every week. I couldn't wait for Saturday nights to go to the club and hear him play his latest, he was so very good at it, I just sat spellbound, I had been at Dutton's for two months now.

One Saturday he surprised me by saying in the middle of his act: 'Ladies and gentlemen – you must have noticed at our table a young good-looking blond gentleman.' All eyes turned towards me and I was looking at lots of smiling eyes. 'His name is Harry – and Harry does a fair old song – I'm sure if we gave him a little bit of encouragement, he'd come up here and give you "Blue Spanish Eyes".' There was some scattered applause and voices saying: 'Good old Harry boy.' Daphne winked and said: 'Sock it to 'em, Harry.'

I trembled, I had never sung in public before. I wanted to but at the same time I didn't want to. It had sounded good when we did it at Jim's house but in a hall this size I didn't know how to go about it. I got up awkwardly and walked towards the stage – I tripped up the only two steps I had to climb. On the milkround, I climbed hundreds of stairs a day loaded with bottles and groceries, yet here I was falling arse over head on two stairs. The audience believed I did it on purpose and laughed.

Jim began to pick out an introduction. I stood near the microphone and sang, it was as quiet as when Jim played his solos, all eyes were on me and most of them were smiling at me, I sang 'Spanish Eyes'. When I finished I was astounded to hear this loud applause and shouts for 'more' amongst it. I tried to walk off the stage but they wouldn't have it. 'Give us another one Harry!' 'One more, please!' I looked at Jim, Jim grinning widely said: 'What you going to do Englebert?' I shrugged. 'Try, "You only have to Smile",' he said over the applause. I sang the words Jim had taught me.

> You only have to smile
> And in a little while
> The world seems to change
> In such a wonderful way
>
> You only have to stand there
> And summertime is here
> Then all those things that flutter by
> The birds and bees and butterflies
> Are singing songs of summer.
> You only have to smile
> That's all you have to do
> The clouds disappear – the sun shines though.
>
> Suddenly, there's music
> It's like a symphony
> The violins begin
> The trumpeters join in
> I hear the angels sing
> When you smile at me.

There was applause, not the sort of applause I had got for 'Spanish Eyes' – this was firm, solid applause, the sort of applause you hear when they give a deserved award on TV – solid handclapping – it was obvious we had moved the audience emotionally, it was a great feeling.

I couldn't wait for Saturdays to come round. I had the bug, I learned more of Jim's songs, I was a quick learner and could usually sing one of his compositions after three or four hearings. I had found out how to modulate my voice, I started listening intently to Frank Sinatra and Jack Jones. I remembered reading somewhere that when Tony Bennett sang a ballad, he pretended the microphone was a girl's ear just four inches away from him. I tried this technique and it worked. All Jim's songs were tender love songs and stood up to this treatment well.

One Saturday evening after we had been doing this for almost three months. I arrived at Jim's house, took my jacket off and young Sheila hung it up. Daphne brought in the tea things and as we all began to tuck in, she suddenly said: 'What have I got in my hand?' Her hands were behind her back. 'A cake,' said Andrew. 'No,' said Daphne. 'Try again.' Jim said, 'A horse and cart.' 'No!' she said, 'it's a letter.'

'How frolicsome,' said Jim.

'A letter from a TV company.'

'Ooh,' said Jim, 'do they want you for *This is Your Life*?'

'No, they don't want me – they want you – you and Harry.' Jim and me looked at each other but said nothing. Daphne was now all quite excited. 'I wrote to *Opportunity Knocks* asking for an audition for you two – I wrote four weeks ago to Teddington and this letter is for you to go to Thames Television and audition next Sunday.' All of us at the same time said: 'Next Sunday?' 'Next Sunday,' she said, her eyes popping. She handed Jim the letter, he read it, looked up and said: 'What made you do that?'

'Because I think you two are very good and I think that you could give a lot more pleasure to a lot more people than you do at the Southwood Social.'

We all looked at her as if she had gone potty, the kids included. She went on.

'Don't let me down, the both of you – I've promised to be your sponsor.'

'Do you think we're good enough, Jim?' I asked. Daphne and the kids all chorused together: 'Yes!' Jim seemed amused: 'Well, if we're not – they'll soon flippin' well tell us so – yeah – why not – let's have a go.'

It was decided we would 'have a go'. The following week, I went over to Jim's house every evening while the kids did their homework. I tried different ways of phrasing, we bought a tape recorder and had great fun letting the kids hear themselves reproduced on tape.

I couldn't keep my mind on my work all through that week – I was messing up orders, leaving eggs where I should have left yoghurts, gold-top where I should have put silver. We didn't even bother to go to the club on the Saturday, we just worked on what we were going to do at our audition.

On Sunday morning, Daphne, Jim and I boarded a train to Teddington and found our way to the TV studios. We showed our letter at the gate to the commissionaire, he showed us through to a studio where about another hundred people were waiting. A little man with a beard came forward and told us we would hear our name called, then we were to go to a part of the floor where a camera would be trained on us. We would be expected to perform for no longer than three minutes – after the act, we were to leave the big studio we were in and wait outside, it was imperative we remained quiet.

The three of us sat in a row of seats with several others. We watched a fellow play a trumpet, a group that had difficulty making the amplification work, there was a conjurer who was so nervous he messed up every trick he did, there were four girl singers who all sang, 'Everything's coming up Roses,' and then a fellow with earphones came towards the audience and shouted: 'Lloyd?' Jim put his hand up. 'Get ready,' he called, 'next!'

Jim got his guitar out of the case and I followed him. 'Any props?' said the fellow with the earphones. 'Any what?' 'Do you need anything?' Jim said very timidly: 'A chair, please.'

There was a fellow in front of us who had been whistling, 'In a monastery garden', as he finished we were ushered in. Jim sat on the chair, a microphone was put near his guitar, the lights came up and a big microphone on what I think they call a boom came towards me. 'Give us a level,' shouted Earphones.

Jim played something on his guitar and after a few seconds a technician came forward and moved the mike closer to Jim's guitar.

'Okay,' said Noddy in the earphones, 'give.' Jim played an introduction and we did 'You only have to smile'. I was amazed how composed I was, I didn't shake or feel nervous. I just sang. It was surprising not to hear any applause because they always applauded at the club. 'Thank you, Mr Lloyd,' said a voice over a speaker. 'Next please.' We tiptoed back to our seats and sat down.

'How was it?' I said to Daphne.

'I could hardly hear you,' she said.

'Come on – let's go!' Jim was ready to leave.

There was a fire-eater on next – when he had finished a voice boomed: 'Is Mr Lloyd there, please?' 'Yes!' Jim shouted back to the intercom. 'I'm here!'

Back came Earphones and told us to go to a small room just at the back of the studio. There, a girl at a desk informed us that we were liked by the people up in the glass booth and we would be hearing from them in the next few weeks. They thanked us for coming and we left.

We were in a shocked state. Daphne had told us she could hardly hear us from about fifteen feet away, yet the powers that be had told us we would be hearing from them soon. We could only guess that those microphones were a lot more powerful than we imagined.

We decided they weren't all that keen on what we had done and to soften the blow they had told us we would be hearing from them.

By Wednesday, we had given up. I had finished the round, Jim and I had our usual pint and I went home to have a kip, for some reason I felt very tired.

The old lady was in as it was summer, the kids were on holiday and she wasn't required to cook school meals. Benjy was there and I knew as soon as I walked in I was an unwelcome visitor but I thought, 'Sod 'em – I've been working.' I cooked a couple of lamb chops and did some of those mashed potatoes you pour boiling water on. The old lady didn't even get up out of her chair. Benjy smoked his dung heap and Jimmy Young rambled like a raped virgin on Radio Two. Above the din, she took the cigarette out of her mouth to say: 'Haven't seen much of you lately.'

'No,' I said. 'I've been delivering milk.'

'You going on with that job?'

'Yeah – I like it.'

'You ought to give a bit more up here.'

'I give you eight quid a week now.'

'It's not enough – rates have gone up – food's gone up – electric – everything.'

'All right, I'll give you an extra couple of quid.'

'That's not much out of forty quid,' said Benjy.

'I don't get forty quid – I have insurance and tax to pay – some weeks I don't make thirty quid.'

'Well, your mother's right – things are more expensive and there's two mouths to feed.'

I was getting fed up with this joker telling me how to live, I decided there and then to put a stop to him.

'More like three mouths to feed.'

'What d'ye mean?' he asked.

'Well – you're never out of here, are you? If we didn't have you round so often there'd be more for us.'

'Harry Selfridge,' said the old lady disbelievingly.

'Well, it's true, ain't it? Three times last week he had eggs and bacon – he's here at weekends eating all that's given to him – I'm not. I have one meal a day here – what am I doing – subsidising *him*.' I pointed with my finger as I said, 'Him.'

They both stared but made no sound. 'Look,' I said, 'I didn't ask to be bloody well born – you were having your fun when I was conceived – you made a mess out of your marriage – now here you are wooing Mister Saint Bruno there – who comes round every bloody day stinking the house out with that pipe and then you tell me to start helping the family budget – I have to spend a tenner in cafés for grub, I have to buy my own clothes and then cough up to keep you and him – if you really want to save, tell him to piss off 'cos if he doesn't, I will.'

I walked into the bedroom and slammed the door. I had no need to blow up but something was bugging me, I didn't know what. I lay on the bed to try to find out what it was that had made me blow my top, I couldn't come up with the answer.

When I woke, it had gone five – there was no activity from the living room – no radio – no TV on. I guessed they must have gone out, my mind went back to the storm a few hours earlier. I had always bottled up my feelings, to take it out on the old lady was cowardly. I sorted out what I was annoyed about – it was not hearing from the *Opportunity Knocks* audition – it hurt to feel you could tear an audience up in one place and not be able to do it elsewhere. I shrugged it off and made a mental note to buy the old lady a packet of fags, this was an effort for me because I dislike smoking. I had once wandered into a cinema up West when they showed what smoking can do to the lungs. I made up my mind then never to give it a whirl. I have known mates I've been with, go berserk for a fag at two o'clock in the morning – I've seen them walk streets looking for a machine to put money in. I've got one mate I see up at the Tavern – you've seen nicotine on somebody's fingers? This fellow's got a segregated hand, his name is Charlie Henderson, he is never without a fag, he once told me he smoked right from the early days, he told me that he was the only kid in the street that had a fire extinguisher in his pram. He collects coupons, he showed me a wristwatch he got for ten thousand of these cigarette coupons – I think it was ten, it might have been twenty thousand – it's hard to tell 'cos he speaks through his cough.

While I was thinking all this, I had wandered into the kitchen. I was about to butter myself a piece of toast when there was a loud rat-tat on the door. I opened it to see Jim Lloyd standing there, his eyes were wide with excitement, he had a telegram in his hand.

'We're on next Sunday!' He thrust the telegram in my hand. It asked Jim to ring a Mr Martin at Thames TV for talks about appearing on *Opportunity Knocks* the following week.

'They liked us!' he yelled. 'We might be rich one day,' he laughed. Jim had come all the way from Southwood to bring me the news. I put my coat on and we walked up to the Tavern, it had just opened, it was five-thirty – by seven o'clock, we were both pissed.

We didn't tell anybody at Dutton's yard next morning.

Both of us had terrible hangovers, it wasn't until later in the day mine cleared up. I felt fragile and was glad to get back to the yard, clear up and go home.

As I turned to get some empties from the float, I found myself looking into the eyes of Eileen Dutton. It was a bright summer's day – she wore a lemon coloured dress, it was tasteful and set her colouring off a real treat.

'Good morning Miss,' I said. I noticed my heart began beating twice as fast.

'Good morning, Harry,' she smiled. 'Everything all right?'

'Yes thanks, Miss.' Sod it, I knew I was blushing. I pretended it was the lifting of the crates making me red and felt for my handkerchief to wipe my face.

She asked me about a customer who had been dodging the bill for the past six weeks, she told me to leave no more milk until they had paid. I made a note in my book to do that, then she said: 'Lovely day.'

'Beautiful day, miss – lovely for a cruise up the river.'

'Do you do that, Harry?'

'I went a couple of times last year – have you ever been miss?'

'I've never thought about it.'

'Oh, you'd love it – you know, all those bridges we go over every day: Albert, Vauxhall, Chelsea?'

She nodded. 'Well – they're works of art when you view them from the river – all their beauty is at water level.'

'Really?'

'Yes, really – Londoners walk about with their noses on the ground, we have got some of the finest architecture in the world here.'

She smiled as I said, 'You ought to go round and see it – I'll take you.'

'I'd love to Harry.'

'If you really would, Miss Dutton, Sunday's the best

day – it's quiet – you don't have to keep jumping out of the way of the traffic.'

'All right, Harry – we'll do that one Sunday.'

I would have asked her there and then to come the following Sunday but I suddenly remembered *Opportunity Knocks* so I just said: 'Okay miss – when you get time.' She flashed me a big smile and went towards the office.

5

The following Sunday, I caught a bus over to Jim's house. When I arrived there was great activity – Daphne had the ironing board out and was ironing the shirt that Jim had decided to wear – somebody had told him that white 'flares' up to the cameras and leaves a haze so he had decided to wear a blue striped one – this was the one Daphne was ironing. I was wearing my Chester Barrie suit and had decided against a tie. Jim had gone out the day before and had a short back and sides at the local barbers, he looked clean and neat, like he had stepped out of a 'B' picture starring John Payne. I'd had my hair washed and blown and felt confident.

A neighbour had offered to drive us over in his car, so with Daphne, Jim, myself and the two neighbours, Jack and Edie Roberts, we left for Teddington Studios – the kids all stood round the car shouting, 'Good luck!' and 'Hope you're not nervous', 'Make sure you win!' Another neighbour was looking after the three kids and as the car took it slowly up Meadow Road, the three of us were looking back waving at them until they disappeared from sight.

'Well – we're off,' said Jim.

'Did you put the guitar in?' asked Daphne.

'Yeah – it's in the boot.'

'Wouldn't it be good if you came first?' she smiled.

'That means you have to go on the following week,' Jim said thoughtfully.

'That'd be nice,' said Mrs Roberts.

'Do you get paid?' said Mr Roberts.

'I dunno,' said Jim – 'nobody's mentioned anything – I s'pose they give you expenses.'

While all this chatter was going on, I suddenly had a sickly feeling come over me – at first, I thought it must be because I was sitting in the back of the car but it wasn't – for the first time it dawned on me what I was doing. A few months had gone past since the start of the job at Dutton's – I had met Jim, done a few songs to his guitar accompaniment, had a few appearances before a friendly audience, now here I am heading towards a television studio to take part in a competitive show where we would be against quite a lot of professional people, or some darn good amateurs. I had seen the show quite often and marvelled at the high standard of the performers, some were better than the professionals who got highly paid for things they did not do as well. We were going to be seen by millions.

'Christ,' I thought. I mopped my brow which had become quite moist, Jim saw me and smiled.

'Nervous, mate?'

'A little bit – you?'

'It doesn't matter so much with me, all I have to do is play the bloody guitar – you've got to sing.'

'He'll be all right,' said Daphne reassuringly.

I tried to make things seem normal to get ourselves out of the nervous state we were heading for.

'Look,' I said, 'it's all a bit of fun, if they like us – OK – if they don't, what have we lost? A Sunday off and half a gallon of petrol.'

'Right,' said Jim.

'Right,' said Daphne.

'Petrol's bloody dear,' said Jack Roberts, we all laughed as he drove us towards our fate.

41

The studios at Teddington were much quieter than the time before, we were allowed into the car park, then we walked along the back of the studios to admire the river. We were told there was a restaurant open, we could use it until we heard our names called over the speakers, then we were to report to Studio A.

Almost as soon as we sat down to drink a cup of tea, our names were called. Then a young fellow with a clipboard in his hand called us towards him, he led us out of the restaurant across a large yard, up some stairs to a very large studio, much bigger than the one we had been in before.

There were rows of seats for about five hundred people; batteries of lights shining down from the high ceiling; four large cameras with Thames on the side, numbered 1, 2, 3 and 4. A fellow with earphones kept shouting out, then retracting a large arm-like sort of thing called a 'boom' with a microphone on the end, I had learned its name last time round. I had some silly joke going through my mind that if he shot it out far enough and it smashed somebody in the face, the fellow at the other end would hear it go, 'Boom!'

The fellow with the clipboard kept listening to his headphones and murmuring things like: 'Uh-uh – Can do – Got it – OK Roger.' Then he took hold of me, positioned me on a high stool, which somebody marked with red tape on the ground. This, I found out, was for when the show was going to be transmitted and would save the scene shifters looking for the spot to 'place' me.

Jim was put about two feet behind me with his guitar 'miked' up. There were shouts of 'Quiet!' and 'Absolute Quiet!' When the whole studio was as quiet as a church, the fellow with the clipboard brought his hand down like he was starting a race and hissed: 'Go!'

Jim played the introduction to 'Spanish Eyes' and I

sang, as I finished on a soft note, a voice boomed through the large speakers: 'Very nice – is Bob Orchestra there?' The leader of the band came forward and yelled up to the boom: 'What is it?'

The voice boomed again: 'It's a bit insipid with just the guitar – would you have time to add a few strings for the second chorus?'

'I think so – we already have an orchestration in the library – I'll check if it's in the same key.'

'Thanks chum,' said the voice: 'Next please.'

The orchestra leader took us to a piano and played what we had just sung and told us he was adding orchestration to give the song some colour. We could go and rehearse with them at two o'clock. As it was only half-past twelve, we were told we could use the bar or restaurant but to be back at two.

Off we went, we pointed to pictures of all the stars whom the studios had in their current shows. There was Tommy Cooper, Benny Hill and all that crowd on *Love Thy Neighbour*. It was rather thrilling to be given a dressing room that had once been occupied by Tom Jones. We had nothing to hang up in the wardrobe that was there, we washed our hands so as we could use the towel, after all this was over we could at least tell our mates we had washed our hands in the same bowl that Tom Jones had used. To make doubly sure we had a good story, Jim, Jack and me all had a 'slash' in the toilet.

We queued at a self-service counter and gave the lady a chit for the meal. Jack and Edie had to pay, he kept making jokes about cost of petrol – buying his own lunch and how it would have been cheaper for him to have stayed at home – it was all good-natured.

We were made very happy by a young technician who sidled over from another table and said: 'T'riffic! – you look really great on the box – that blond hair – good song

43

– you sing it well – you've got a great chance of winning – t'riffic!'

'Thanks mate,' I said. 'Are you connected with it?'

'Sound, I am, mate – d'ye know what I'm gonna do?'

We all shook our heads.

'I'm gonna give you a little bit of echo – make it sound more plaintive – be great – t'riffic!'

He tucked into a big plate of roast beef, potatoes and cabbage – we all watched him devour it. As he swallowed the last mouthful, he said: 'T'riffic' again, then got up and went.

We watched him go, then we left ourselves. We were taken to a band room that was filled with elderly fellows who were tucking violins under their chins. I don't think there was one of them under fifty, the orchestra leader tapped with his stick and said: 'Right boys.' I thought: 'Boys! Christ, I've seen younger looking Chelsea pensioners.'

The leader brought his stick down and there came the most beautiful sound I think I have ever heard. I couldn't recognise 'Spanish Eyes' but Jim assured me that this was the harmony and as long as I concentrated on what I usually sang, the blending would be great. The leader asked me to try it, I did as he said and suddenly felt marvellous – it was wonderful to sing with Jim's guitar but this was a sound that was unbelievable. The leader put his ear quite near to my lips and said: 'Don't push it – let it come out naturally.' I did and it felt good. As I finished, he patted my arm and said: 'Very nice.'

As we all stood there, a voice came over the speaker: 'Mrs Daphne Lloyd – go to Studio A please.' Daphne turned deep red at hearing her name, all flustered she turned towards the speaker and said: 'Where?' almost as if it heard her, it repeated 'Studio A.'

We left the band room and went to the studio, we

recognised Hughie Green, tall and grey-haired. This was the first time we had seen him, he wore casual clothes and was reading a script. Daphne was brought over to him, he shook her hand and the two of them chatted for three or four minutes. She came back all wide-eyed and said to us: 'He's ever so nice – makes you really at home.'

'What did he ask you?' questioned Jim.

'He wanted to know what time you got up – how many children we have – how long we'd been married – oh, lots of things.'

Suddenly, the floor manager interrupted by yelling 'Stand by all performers – we are going for a run through!' There was a buzz of excitement. He continued: 'All right people – keep it quiet – absolute quiet!'

A man held what looked like a clock in front of a camera and said: 'Opportunity Knocks – take one!' As the hand reached twelve, the band struck up from the band room and the sound was relayed on the big speakers in the studios, over the noise I could hear a voice saying, 'And here is the man himself, Hughie Green!'

Mr Green made his appearance, still in his casual clothes – somebody handed him a microphone, he quietly said: 'So and so and so and so – meet our first sponsor, who is so and so – chat chat, etcetera.' He asked for some words to be written and the floor manager said: 'Right – idiot boards!' Some large boards were produced with words written on them which I couldn't see.

He introduced a group of singers and instrumentalists at the other end of the studio. I was wondering how the audience would ever see them but realised they looked up at the monitors; which were large TV screens; there were about a dozen of these and it was easy to follow the action from them. He then introduced a young girl who played a trumpet, she played it clearly and well. Then somebody said that's where the break came and for me and Jim to 'stand by'.

A red light flashed, the orchestra blared again – Daphne was pushed into a seat beside Mr Green, they chatted quietly while we were ushered to our marks. I heard a voice say, '. . . so for Jim Lloyd and Harry Selfridge – Opportunity Knocks!'

Our song over, the floor manager clapped his hands like a seal, obviously allowing for the time when the real audience came and did what was expected of them.

We watched a man do farmyard impressions, then saw a female singer who had a great voice, similar to Shirley Bassey, sing a song I had never heard before, and, finally, a crowd of operatic singers who did a selection from White Horse Inn.

We were then told to go and have tea, then be in make-up at four o'clock ready to go on the air in front of the audience at four-thirty.

We wandered over to the restaurant and had a cup of tea. The young technician who had spoken to us before was in the canteen, he put his thumb up to us and said : 'T'riffic!' Then ate another big plate of food – bigger than the one we'd seen him eat a couple of hours before.

Jim and I were shown into the make-up department – a girl went to work on each of us. She put a light dusting of dark powder on my skin, then went to work on my eyes, she muttered : 'What lovely lashes' and proceeded to stroke them with a mascara brush.

Jim and me got up out of the chairs, looked at each other and began to laugh : 'I fancy you,' said Jim. 'I'll tell Daphne,' I said. As we were going out, he touched me up the jacksy, we were both giggling like kids, I'm sure it was nerves. 'No wonder you were in the Navy,' I said.

With the audience in their seats, the show took on a new life. Everybody became energetic, a man walked out and did a ten minute 'warm-up' spot, he then introduced Hughie Green, who was now dressed in an immaculate suit, as debonair as we had ever seen him, he told jokes to the audience and got gales of laughter. The audience was made up of mostly elderly people, then, almost before we had time to weigh it all up, the show had begun.

The orchestra played a big fanfare, cameras were coming in close, then going back again, it was as it had been in rehearsal except it had, as I said, 'come to life'.

I heard Hughie Green say: 'Sitting beside me, ladies and gentlemen, is a housewife – will you tell us your name please?'

Daphne swallowed and said: 'Daphne Lloyd.'

'Daphne what? Will you speak up a little bit so the lovely folks at home can hear you.'

'Lloyd – Daphne Lloyd,' she almost shouted.

'What do you do Daphne?'

'I'm a milkman's wife.'

'You're a milkman's wife? Isn't that wunnerful, let's have a bit of applause for all the milkmen's wives in this big wunnerful country of ours.'

There was rapturous applause dutifully supplied. 'Does your husband get up early?'

'Four a.m.'

'Four a.m.? I know a story about a milkman,' said Hughie.

'Is it rude?' said Daphne. I found out afterwards that Daphne had been briefed to say all this.

'Is it what, darling?'

'Is it rude?' Daphne was getting good laughs from the audience – they seemed to like her good humour.

'Have you ever heard a milkman story that wasn't rude?' Another big laugh.

He went on to tell a story about a milkman who was having an affair with a woman and her husband found out, one morning he came home to find the milkman's horse and cart outside, he looked through his window and saw his wife having a bit of slap and tickle with the milkman.

'What did he do?' asked Daphne.

'He walked out of the gate and he didn't 'arf kick his horse.'

I had fallen out of the cradle laughing at that one but the audience roared and gave them another big round of applause.

'Who are you going to introduce to us?' asked Hughie.

'My husband and his mate, Harry Selfridge.'

'Are they both milkmen?'

'Yes, they are both milkmen.'

'All right – ladies and gentlemen, for two milkmen from Southwood, London – Jim Lloyd and Harry Selfridge – Opportunity Knocks!'

There was great applause and the stage manager gave the cue for Jim to start.

In the quiet that followed, Jim played the introduction to 'Spanish Eyes' and I sang. I sang it as well as I could under the circumstances, I wished Jim had been a little nearer to me, I tried not to 'push it' because I could hear myself go out of tune if I did, the boom mike was only two inches from my head, then the violins from the orchestra crept in and I suddenly felt very good, we seemed to be doing well.

There was solid applause at the end and the show continued. At the finale of the show, Hughie Green walked to his clapometer, this board indicates how the studio audience reacts. We came second, the girl with the big voice and Bristols came first. For the final result we would have to wait for the viewers' votes to be counted the following Friday.

A young girl secretary came up to us and asked us if we had another song ready, should we happen to win the vote. All we could think of was Jim's composition, 'You only have to smile'. She said she would be in touch if anything happened. We left feeling elated, coming second wasn't bad! The girl that won was a professional we were told, so we could hold our heads high. Then we left.

The next day was Monday, we were going to see the show that evening as it had been recorded. Once again, I couldn't keep my mind on my work – when I saw Jim, I said: 'I wonder if Cecil B. de Mille will be in touch with us after tonight's show?'

He laughed: 'You got colour?'

'No, black and white.'

'We're going to see it at the Roberts' – they've got colour.'

'I'll watch it at home – I can't wait to see the old lady's face – I haven't told her we're on.'

'You'll have to tell her it's your twin brother.' He chuckled.

I got cleaned up and was about to leave the yard when I saw Eileen Dutton just outside the office – she looked dejected. I walked over to her.

'Anything wrong, Miss?'

She looked up and gave me a weak smile.

'Old Fred's wife has 'phoned up to say he had a heart attack over the weekend.'

'Oh dear,' I said.

'I hope he's going to be all right – we could do with him now – summer holidays coming up and we're so short handed.'

'He'll be fine,' I said. 'Old milkmen never die ...'

'You look after yourself Harry, we don't want to lose any more of our good men.' She smiled and went back to the office.

6

The signal for Thames Television came up. Benjy began to stuff his pipe, the old lady lit up one of her coffin nails and soon there was a blue haze in the room. I walked forward and turned the volume up a shade.

'Going deaf?' said the old lady.

We watched a group, then the farmyard impressionist, then there was a commercial break. Immediately following the break, Hughie Green told us he had a milkman's wife sitting beside him – the picture went to Daphne for the first time and I realised what a good personality she had. They went through the same routine they had done the day before, except that with no other distractions and just their two heads on the screen, it seemed cosier, the laughs seemed much louder than the scattered sound I had heard yesterday. My heart started thumping as if somebody was pounding my chest with a hammer, it was all I could do to stop myself running out of the room. I heard Hughie Green say: '... for two milkmen – Jim Lloyd and Harry Selfridge – Opportunity Knocks!'

'Ooh,' muttered the old lady, 'same name as you.'

I watched the screen dissolve, gradually it cleared then focussed on to the hole in the middle of Jim's guitar, slowly it pulled away to show his hand plucking the strings – as my voice came in, the camera pulled away to show the two of us in a long, far away shot – then it came in slowly for a close up, she muttered again: 'Looks a bit like you, too.'

I stared straight ahead. There was a cut and suddenly my head was filling the screen, they gasped.

'Bloody hell – it is him – it's our Harry,' she said.

'Ssh!' I said. 'Listen.'

'What ...?' said Benjy.

'Listen for Chrissake,' I said. They both sat dumb-
founded.

I had never seen myself like this before, it was different
to looking in a mirror. I blinked and could watch myself
blink. I liked what I saw. My hair was several shades lighter
because of the lighting over my head, when I smiled my
teeth looked good and healthy and the voice seemed firm
and resonant – furthermore, I looked like I was enjoying
what I was doing.

Jim had his head bent over the guitar watching his
left hand as he picked out the chords – he also had a nice
serene look – now and again, he looked at me as if I was
Muhammad Ali, it made a very nice picture. As I finished
the song, there was a burst of applause that seemed to
shake the set.

'I can't believe it,' she said.

'When did you do this Harry?' asked Benjy. He had a
new sort of look on his face.

'Yesterday,' I said.

'Who's the other bloke?'

'He's a pal I work with.'

'Did you win?' asked the old lady.

'No – some girl singer beat us but we have to wait for
the viewers' vote.' I tried to sound nonchalant.

We were interrupted by knocking on the front door –
the old lady in flushed excitement, rushed to open it. It
was Mr and Mrs Dempsey from next door.

'We've just seen you on the box,' blurted out Mr Dempsey.

'Wasn't he good?' said Mrs Dempsey.

'There's a girl coming on now who beat us,' I said.

The room went still as we listened to the girl singer.
She had a powerful voice that seemed to be a bit out of

tune, in the vast studio yesterday it hadn't been so notice-
able, she also grimaced quite a bit and her big notes made
the veins stick out in her neck.

'She's not as good as our Harry,' said the old lady.

'Sounds like a cat pissing on a tin can,' said Mr Dempsey.

'No chance,' said Benjy.

We watched the summing up at the end, then everybody
started talking at once.

'I didn't know he could sing.'

'Didn't he look handsome – looks a bit like Paul Newman.'

'Well, who'd have thought Harry boy was a telly star.'

'I'm not a star – I just did it for a bit of fun,' I laughed.

'You're a lot better than some of that bleedin' rubbish
they put on,' said Mr Dempsey.

In the middle of all this, the old lady said something
she hadn't said for years. She said: 'Would you like a cup
of tea, darling?'

Next morning I arrived fifteen minutes late at the yard.
This was because I had twisted and turned the night
before – the excitement had made it impossible for me to
sleep. The old lady wakened me, what's more, she was up
cooking my breakfast.

As I entered the yard, there were cries of:

'There he is – the answer to Tom Jones.'

'How's Simon and Garfunkel today?'

'Great boys – great.'

There was lots of back slapping – Jim was enjoying it
as much as I was.

'We've made a rod for our backs now, mate,' he laughed.

I began loading, every milkman there seemed to be singing 'Spanish Eyes'.

The dawn had brought a bright summer day, I was

53

glad in a way to get out on the round. As I drove the float over the bridge, I found myself hoping that we would win the following week. It crossed my mind to stop at a post office when they opened, post a card and mark myself and Jim as the winners but dismissed it as cheating.

One of my calls was at a block called Embankment Mansions. It was my practice to put a full crate of milk in the lift and go to the top floor, then I would work my way down to the bottom again, getting lighter.

When I got out at the third, there was a flat door slightly ajar, as I bent down to pick up a couple of empties, I stood up to see a smashing looking bird standing there in a negligent – and I mean negligent – because it was neglecting everything – I didn't know where to look for the best – I had so many choices.

'Hello Harry,' she said, she sounded like that one that does the ads sometimes – I think her name's Fenella Fielding.

'Hello,' I smiled.

'How's our troubadour, today?'

'I'm all right thanks,' I guessed she must have seen the programme the night before.

'What a lovely voice our beautiful milkman has.'

I felt myself reddening.

'Fancy a cup of tea?' She let the negligée hang like a shawl.

'Well I've got a lot to do and I'm a bit late today.' I tried to clear a big frog that had suddenly come up – among other things.

'A cup of tea won't take long,' she said.

I said, 'Okay,' and walked into the apartment.

She took me through to a small kitchen and sat me at a small kitchen table. She started to tell me how good she thought we were the night before. The kettle whistled the signal that it needed unplugging. She poured boiling water

54

into a teapot. While she waited for it to draw, she stood right in front of me and said,

'Let me have a good look at those lashes.'

I put my hands out to stop her toppling over me and it was off!

She had pushed both her breasts in my face – as I fought for breath, her hands became windmills, with her left she stroked my hair, with the right she reached down to where my zip began.

'The bed – the bed,' she gasped. She almost lifted me out of the chair and led me by the hand into a bedroom, the bed was unmade, she let her negligée fall to the ground, flopped on her back, looking up at me she said in a voice that had gone two tones lower: 'You wicked man – you're going to do things to me.'

And I did.

It was on the way back to reload, I suddenly thought, 'Christ, I didn't drink my tea.'

'Hello Harry,' said Eileen Dutton, as I began reloading. She had come out of the office and sidled up to me.

'I hear that two of our best milkmen were on the television.'

'Did you see it, miss?'

'No Harry – I was working here till past eight.'

'Oh, it was just a bit of fun.'

'I hear you were exceptionally good,' she smiled.

'Well – you know.'

'I wish you luck – does it mean you will leave us?'

'No,' I blurted out much too quickly. 'No!'

'I thought you were going to take me and show me London some time.'

'I'd love to.'

'What about Sunday?'

'I'd love to.'

'All right,' she smiled. 'We'll make arrangements later in the week.'

'Yeah – fine – certainly – I'll look forward to it.'

I was just about to say that if we won the vote we would be needed at the studio but it sounded a bit big-headed, I knew we wouldn't really win.

'I'll see you before Friday,' she flashed that great smile and was gone.

It was on the Friday afternoon, I got a telegram asking me to contact the producer of *Opportunity Knocks*. I went down to the 'phone box and called the number they had given me. When I got through I was asked if we could come up with another song. I told them we had, 'You Only Have to Smile' – the one that Jim had composed, he asked me if I could get a top line of the song written out and get it to him – if need be, he would send a messenger to pick it up. I said I would try to organise it.

Jim had given me the Roberts' number which I dialled and asked Mrs Roberts to go and get Jim. He came to the 'phone after I had put a couple of 10p pieces in the coin box. I told him what had been requested. He said he thought he could write one out and he would 'phone them when it was ready, he reckoned he could knock it off in an hour.

The producer said he wasn't quite sure if we had won but it seemed as if we had got more votes than anyone else.

At eight o'clock that night, a telegram arrived telling me we had won the vote and to be at the studio at the same time on Sunday. I telephoned Jim with the news, he was breathless with excitement. The music had gone off and we would have an orchestration ready for Sunday when we arrived.

The next morning, I rang Eileen Dutton to tell her I

wouldn't be able to take her on our trip. She understood and wished me good luck.

It was different at the studios this Sunday. We knew the geography of the place and had learned a little of the technical jargon and procedure. With the new contestants, we were able to point out the canteen, the dressing-rooms, the make-up department. We were gazed at in a knowing way and were treated by the others as celebrities, one young girl came up and asked me for my autograph – I wrote: 'Best wishes – Harry Selfridge,' in her autograph book, she looked at it and said: 'What – no kisses?'

I put a couple of crosses and she went off smiling.

It was the first time I had ever been asked for my autograph – I liked it – I began to hope we would win tonight's show.

We were announced as the winners by Hughie Green – the audience applauded loudly and long, we stood there awkwardly basking in the adulation.

'What will it be this week, boys?' asked Hughie Green.

'We have written a song, it's called, "You Only Have To Smile",' said Jim.

'Who wrote the words and who wrote the music?'

'He wrote the words and the music,' I said, pointing at Jim.

'But he just said a song we had written – where do *you* come in?'

'I lent him the pencil,' I said.

There was a big laugh from the audience, Mr Green was quite unprepared for it, I didn't mean to be funny, it just came out. I was not quite sure whether he was pleased or not at my off-the-cuff remark, but after pursing his lips, he broke into a smile and said: 'All right, for our two milk-men from London, Jimmy Lloyd and Harry Selfridge – Opportunity Knocks!'

The fellow from the sound department gave us a thumbs up as we left and another. 'T'riffick'. We made for home, two of the happiest human beings in the whole world. Even Mr Roberts was singing, 'You Only Have To Smile', as we drove towards Southwood.

7

Solomon Segal, Theatrical Agent. Read the sign outside the dingy office just off Regent Street.

Solly had wandered into the agency business direct from the Army where he had been conscripted for two years. At an Army concert he had been lucky enough to see a quartet of soldiers who had modelled themselves on Bill Haley's Comets, they played the same tunes in the same way that the famous rock and roll band played them. He had made quite a good living from them since the mid-fifties.

With the coming of the Beatles, the group who called themselves the Rockolas had become old hat. Solly had booked a few clubs for the Rockolas but slowly, as the boys in the group had gone different ways, the group had disintegrated. The teenagers had become uninterested, they didn't draw any more and Solly was looking for a meal ticket to replace them.

He sat this evening gazing at the Regent Street traffic, wondering why he was never lucky enough to find himself a Tom Jones or an Elton John. He read in one of the trade papers that Tom Jones had just done a film deal in Hollywood at a figure exceeding one million dollars, as he slowly broke this down mentally from dollars to pounds and estimated ten per cent, the phone rang.

It was a request from a pub in Kingston asking what sort of price he was asking for the Rockolas for a Saturday night appearance.

'The boys are in great demand,' he lied.

'Could you give us some idea of their fee?' asked the voice.

'They couldn't do it under a hundred and fifty quid.'

'Oh – we were looking for something about sixty quid.'

'Look,' said Solly, 'leave me your number, I'll talk to them and come back to you.'

The voice gave a number which Solly hastily wrote on his pad. He then picked up the 'phone and dialled Sticks Murray, the leader of the Rockolas.

'Sticks? I've got a job for you – it's only forty quid but you ought to do it.'

'Where is it?' asked Sticks.

'Kingston.'

'Forty quid ain't much.'

'Look Sticks, money is tight – you might as well do this as sit around on a Saturday night.'

'But forty quid – that don't hardly pay for petrol.'

'Look if you don't want it – I'll offer it to someone else.'

'All right,' said Sticks, 'we'll do it – but when you gonna get us some real work with real money – I'm fed up with these pissholes we keep going to.'

'I'm working on it Sticks – I'm working – I'm hoping to fix you six months at a nice holiday camp this summer – just leave it with me – I'll call you.'

Solly hung up and dialled the Kingston pub.

'Hello,' he said smilingly – 'I've just had a word with Mr Murray and he has decided to help you out – he will do it for seventy.'

There was a half-hearted argument from the other end.

'Look friend – the Rockolas are a big act, they are giving up an engagement in Newcastle just to stay off the M1, they have been exhausting themselves driving up and down – you are getting a lovely deal at seventy quid, say yes and I'll confirm it.'

The party must have given him the affirmative, he replaced the phone and wiped a bead of sweat from his brow. This was the only job he had fixed this week. He made the contract out for seventy pounds to be paid direct to Segal's Agency. He would give the group forty, collect four pounds commission and not mention that he was selling them for seventy – after all, he was what the profession now calls management. Those ten percenter days were behind. He was looking for an act he could manage and *he* would pay the salary to *them* after he had accepted the deal on *his* terms. It was only a question of time – one day, he told himself, he would walk into a pub or concert or club, and there would be the new Englebert Humperdinck. He went out most nights searching for somebody with the magic of a Tommy Steele or Shirley Bassey. If he, or she, should be green all the better, *he'd* make them into a star.

He had that belief, he knew it was just a question of time. It was late as he decided to leave the office, he glanced at his wristwatch, it was after half past six – he decided to give the traffic a little longer and avoid the rush, he'd watch a bit of *Opportunity Knocks*. He switched on the black and white set he kept in his office.

The show had already begun – he was in time to hear the names of Jimmy Lloyd and Harry Selfridge announced.

He watched as the camera dwelled on Harry singing, 'You Only Have to Smile'.

He liked what he saw – a light-haired, good-looking young man, clean cut with an infectious smile that played around the corners of his mouth, the eyes were bright with long lashes.

His partner was okay, being okay made the younger one more of a stand-out. The TV people had realised this and placed him a foot or two behind the one now singing.

Solly watched until they finished, heard the applause and wondered what lucky agent had managed to sign them up – this was star material if ever he had seen it. He was just about to switch off when a thought struck him. What if by some chance they were *not* represented by an agency.

He looked up the number of the TV company and dialled. A voice answered. Solly knew he would not be given the 'phone number of the contestants so he decided to play it casually.

'I wonder if you can help me?' he asked plausibly. 'I have just been watching *Opportunity Knocks* and saw my brother on there. We were parted when we were kids, I haven't seen him all these years – his name is Harry Selfridge – have you got an address for him, or telephone number?'

'Hang on,' said the man at the other end.

After a couple of minutes the voice returned.

'He ain't got a telephone number but his address is sixty-eight Epsom Flats – sixty-eight – Epsom Flats – Battersea.'

Solly thanked him and noted the address.

Solomon Segal looked at his watch, saw it was not yet eight o'clock and steered his car towards the Embankment, he glanced across the river towards the power station belching four columns of smoke that met in the still air to remind him of the pictures he had seen at various times of the atom bomb explosion – they referred to it as a mushroom cloud and this seemed very similar.

He also reminded himself that somewhere amongst that fallout was one Harry Selfridge, who probably didn't know it but would one day be very wealthy, if he had the right sort of management. He got an uncontrollable urge to turn left and cross Albert Bridge.

He spun the wheel and did that, he stopped first at a garage for petrol. He asked the attendant if he knew of Epsom Flats. The attendant pointed to a high rise block towards the river edge. Solly paid him and drove towards the towering building.

He stopped the Mini outside and thought for a while. It was possible that he might be first – perhaps there was no other agent handling Harry Selfridge, what if he could get him to sign a contract making him the sole agent, perhaps, perhaps ...

Solly left the car double parked and wandered into the square, there seemed to be dozens of kids kicking footballs, playing cricket or skipping.

Sixty-eight was on the ninth floor. He pressed the elevator button, the doors closed and immediately he was aware of the smell of disinfectant.

He stepped out on the ninth and walked towards the door that had sixty-eight on in white plastic numerals. He looked for a bell but could not find one, he banged on the knocker.

Mrs Selfridge answered the door with an enquiring look.

Solly, whose first job after being demobbed was to sell household brushes, knew a thing or two about charming the ladies.

'Is your brother Harry in?'

'Harry? Harry's my son.'

'No – you're joking.' His eyes were disbelieving, 'You're not Harry's *mother*.'

'Yes I am,' she preened.

'Good heavens – I'm Solomon Segal.' He said it like he would have said, 'I'm Florenz Ziegfeld.'

'Who?' said Lil Selfridge.

'I'm Solomon Segal – the impresario – is Harry in?'

'Yes, he is,' Lil was most impressed. 'Come in.'

Solomon walked into the tiny flat, there was Benjy, Mr

and Mrs Dempsey and Harry sitting round a tiny coffee table that had four quart bottles of light ale on. They were all drinking. As he entered, they stopped talking and looked up.

I had been feeling good, I had watched myself on *Opportunity Knocks*. We had opened a few quarts of ale, I was just getting the taste when the old lady walked in with this geezer with frizzy hair, thick glasses and a moustache that made him look like Groucho Marx, he must have been in his mid thirties. There was a strong smell of after-shave hovering about him. He smelt like a knocking shop. As I was trying to decide whether he was a poof or not, he spoke.

'You're Harry Selfridge.'

I honestly spun round to see if there was anybody else.

'What a great pleasure this is, Harry.'

I cleared the haze that was in my eyes by blinking three or four times as I focussed, he was shaking my hand like a village pump handle.

'It's a long time since anybody moved me like you did,' he said.

'Me?'

'Yes, you – you and your mate the guitarist.'

'Jimmy Lloyd?'

'That's his name – Jimmy – great – the pair of you.'

'He is great,' I grinned.

'Your manager must be proud of you.'

'What manager?'

'Don't tell me you don't have a manager!'

(Solly could hardly conceal the rush of blood that went to his head at that moment)

'No, we don't have no manager – we don't need managers – milkmen don't!'

'You are right – milkmen do not, but superstars do. I

don't think you know how big you are going to be Harry – you need a manager to guide you – with the right guidance, you could be a great act, giving pleasure to millions.'

I liked the way he put that – it would be nice to give pleasure to people, but how?

'Where do we find a manager?' I asked him.

'I *might* do it,' said Solly whats'is name.

The old lady let out a whoop and examined the card he had given her as he walked in, she read out: 'Startime Promotions.' Everybody else either went 'Ooh!' or 'Ah!'

'I could start you two boys at two hundred pounds a week – all you'd have to do is fifteen minutes every night.'

'Where?'

'All over the place – I book all the class clubs, I could get you even more if you'd like to throw in a few Sunday concerts.' He looked casual. 'Nearer three hundred.'

Everybody whistled, me included.

'Three hundred?'

(Solly had already worked out that an *Opportunity Knocks* winner of two weeks or more could command a salary of five hundred a week at one of the northern clubs.)

'You'd have to pay me ten per cent,' he laughed.

They all laughed, the old lady said: 'Harry, you're a star.'

8

Jimmy and I both signed a contract with Solly Segal, this made him our manager and for all monies he earned for us, we paid him thirty per cent.

We had won every *Opportunity Knocks* for the past five weeks, it was amazing how people recognised us in the streets, especially if we were together, they'd shout out things like 'Good luck to you!' 'You deserve it.' 'Keep it up!' Nobody seemed to resent us, the milk round was taking twice as long to do because customers were waiting at their doors to chat me up. I thought at the time, 'the bleedin' nation must spend their time looking at that goggle box.'

The birds that looked like scrubbers, were suddenly coming to the door with fresh make-up on and newly combed hair, all of them wanted to know if I fancied a cup of tea. I had so much tea one morning I had to take ten 'leaks', usually I only went once on a round.

It was all coming very easy; when I mentioned to Jim how the crumpet stakes had improved, he confessed he was having the same problems.

The morning before he'd just put a couple of pints outside this divorcee's house, as he stood up, she was standing there in the usual 'come on' attire, see-through nightdress, casually open at the front, she gave him the eye, asked him if he fancied a cup of tea, before he could say no, she had him inside, door locked with a cup of quick brew all ready.

Before he could say, 'I'm not that sort of fellow,' – he was! She was down on the settee all ready for Jim to ride her. He pushed all thoughts of Daphne from his mind –

got on top of her, then suddenly – Wallop! On top of him jumped her Great Dane dog. The dog started riding him, she starts shouting, 'Down boy!' Jim can't move because the dog has got them both pinned down, his jowls are slobbering, the dog's not Jim's, he is panting like a pair of bellows. Jim's stand goes down with a rush, he somehow manages to get off, says goodbye to the dame, runs up the road, gets on with his round. His next call is at the vestry door of the vicarage, the vicar's wife who always chats to him, takes her two pints and slams the door in his face – as Jim tries to figure out what he has done to upset her, he looks down to find his flies wide open and his striped shirt sticking out.

I was still drying the tears of laughter from my eyes when I saw Solomon Segal at the end of the yard – he was frantically waving to us, we left the crates and walked towards him.

'I think it was your lucky day when I booked you two,' he gloated.

'What's the good news, Solly?' Jim asked.

'Your first record.'

'A record?' We both said it together.

'For Lantern Records – a three year contract – five per cent of all sales – your record, "You Only Have to Smile" – put "Lover Boy" on the B side – if this clicks, we could be splitting ten thousand pounds!'

'Ten thousand pounds!' I whistled.

'If it clicks – it could too – there have been dozens of enquiries all round the country from people asking for it at record shops.'

'Ten thousand pounds,' said Jim, still in a daze. 'When do we do it?'

'That's what I came for – tomorrow afternoon, we've booked the band, the singers, and the studio, all you boys have to do is be at Baker Street by two o'clock – don't be late because those musicians cost blood – this little lot is costing the company a couple of grand – so, as I say – don't be late!'

We took the address he had scribbled down. Solly jumped into his small car and was gone.

As we watched the car go down the road, Jim turned to me and said: 'What are you going to do with your three thousand?'

I said: 'Buy another dick – this one's worn out!'

Then I jumped on his back and did a fairly good impression of a Great Dane.

So we had survived as winners for five weeks; we'd had some pretty stiff competition but somehow the cards that came in voted us tops. It was impossible to walk in the street and not be recognised, if I walked into a pub for a drink with the lads, people kept pushing a drink towards me, it was impossible to pace my drinking like I had before. I had been able to have a slow drink from seven until closing time before I had become 'a face', now I was pissed before an hour had passed. The hangovers from this were murder, so I gave it the elbow and stopped going to the pub, if I did relent I never went out until an hour before they call time. That way, I could keep the beer in check.

Another strange thing that happened was that people I used to have a half a pint of bitter with, suddenly decided that because I was on television, I should be drinking spirits and without asking me what my preference was, they stuck a whisky or gin in my hand. I drank them to please, but my head was going round like a spinning top after a couple. I wasn't enjoying it.

I overslept on two mornings, and had to move like a scalded cat to catch up on the round.

Our record was out in the shops. It was being played

almost every hour on some radio programme or another, we had been on *Top of the Pops*, we did interviews with DJs, we were informed that we were now in the Top Twenty.

Solly had a telephone put in the flat and that seemed to be ringing all day long.

Jim Lloyd also had a telephone installed and we called each other three or four times a day. We had no need to but he was the only other person I knew with a telephone apart from Solly. It gave me a kick to dial the number and say to Jim: 'Selfridge 'ere – can I speak to Lloyd?'

For some reason Solly called *me* with all the news then, in turn I relayed it to Jim. Solly assumed I was the business side of the partnership so that when he talked contracts, money or engagements, he came through to me. Jim accepted this as I lived nearer to Solly's Regent Street office. Mostly, when there were contracts to sign, Solly motored over to Battersea and left the documents with me. Jim added his signature the following day, then Solly came out to pick them up.

It was during that fifth week, Solly arrived with his eyes as bright as the early autumn sun that was up in the sky.

'I think you two boys' days as milkmen are over,' he said.

'Why Sol?' I had shortened his name because it gave me a smile inside. Every time he got us a deal, I had cracked to Jim, 'Sol music'. It was an inside joke that we both liked.

He produced a contract.

'This is for *one* week at Bristol – at the Hippodrome – second top to Billy Bassett – four hundred pounds a week.'

'Four hundred?' We stared disbelievingly.

'Four hundred – that's about twice as much as the Prime Minister makes in a week.'

'When?'

'Next week – for six days.'

'What about our jobs?' asked Jim.

'They'll just have to find somebody else, won't they?' laughed Solly.

'Wait a minute,' said Jim. 'We just can't go to Bristol next week and leave the guv'nor – just like that – can we Harry?'

'Well-er – no,' I agreed.

Sol let the grin slide from his face.

'Now look boys – are you going to be milkmen or are you going to be performers, making a couple of grand a week? I mean say so now – I mean – I mean look ...' He began to sound like Alf Garnett.

'I mean to say – I've been working ten hours a day for you lads. It was *me* that got that record of yours in the Top Twenty – that has got to bring you in at least five grand – what is this – what goes on?'

'Nothing goes on,' said Jim. 'We happen to work for a firm that treats us all right – we wouldn't like to let them down – that's all.'

Sol said: 'Look, you take a week off – see if you get over with the public – how do you know whether they'll like you live, you might be horrible, I fixed you this week for you to try it – look – if you were sick they'd have to manage, wouldn't they?'

He answered his own question – ' 'Course they would.'

'We could have a talk with them,' I said.

'That's it, Harry – tell them you've got a contract – see if you like it – look, at this performing lark, you're not out in all weathers giving yourself pneumonia, are you? You're not up at five o'clock every morning climbing stairs, carrying crates of back bleedin' milk are you? – Christ, what do I have to do to you two – when I left the office with this contract, I thought you'd both kiss me for what I'd done for you – I didn't anticipate me standing here

begging you to accept the chance of a lifetime. Christ —
I'm — I'm speechless.'

Solly looked like a goldfish we once had, if we tapped
gently on the side of the bowl before we fed him, he
would come to where your fingertips were, then look
heavenwards for the feed that we'd drop in.

We both stood there shamefaced. I was the first to
speak:

'Let's give it a try, Jim — you might enjoy it.'

'Okay — but who's going to tell the guv'nor?'

'I'll tell her,' I said.

We took the contract from Solly and signed where he
had put two pencil crosses. He stuffed the contract in his
pocket, took his top handkerchief out to wipe his brow,
got in his car and disappeared. I thought again of the
goldfish, after he had got what he wanted it didn't matter
how much you tapped on the side, he couldn't have cared
less — not until next feeding time.

We walked down the yard towards the office.

'Don't forget to tell her it's just for a week,' said Jim.

It was Monday morning. The theatre at Bristol was like a
mausoleum, from the stage we looked at tier upon tier of
empty seats. I felt a tremble go through me as I imagined
those same seats full of people for the evening performance.

The musicians were sorting out what I had learnt were
their 'dots'. A stage manager was giving orders to some
men in the 'flys', he 'tied off', that is he hung different
coloured cloths on some steel bars, I watched them ascend
towards the roof. Lights of all colours were being switched
on and off, a young fellow was feeding out cable from the
various microphones towards a control box on the side of
the stage.

The top-of-the-bill star, Billy Bassett, entered in a loud

check overcoat, dark sunglasses were perched on the top of his head, he looked about forty-five. His Barnet was going but a clever hairdresser had brought it over from the back and made it look quite plentiful.

Somebody must have told him we were the act from *Opportunity Knocks* and would be supporting him all week.

He walked towards Jim and me, then held out a weak wet limp hand.

'How are you?' He didn't bother to introduce himself, he assumed we had seen him enough on the box. Jim answered first:

'Very well, thank you, Mr Bassett.'

'We're all going to be one happy family this week – aren't we?'

'Yes,' I stammered.

'We've always loved you on the old telly,' said Jim.

'Thank you,' he was talking to Jim but he was looking at me.

'You make my mum laugh,' I said.

'Do I? That's nice!'

I felt a bit of a flush coming up. I'd heard at some time this Billy Bassett was bent and he was looking at me a bit intently. He spoke again.

'Lovely eyelashes – get tonight's performance over and we'll get together – where are you staying?'

'I think it's called the – er – Royal Hotel.'

'Oh good,' said B.B. – he was called this by all his followers.

'Well – er – we most certainly *will* get together.'

He swept out and made towards the dressing-rooms.

'He's got to be an iron hoof,' I whispered to Jim.

'Yes,' said Jim, 'keep your back to the wall, Harry.'

'Did you hear what they call him?' I asked Jim. 'B.B.'

'It can't mean bloody butch,' Jim gave me a quick 'Ssh,'

with his eyes, then Solly called us over to the musicians and we rehearsed our three songs with them.

Solly had taken us both to a West End tailor who had fitted us up with two black dinner suits, they were off-the-peg and were not a bad fit. I thought they made us look a bit sombre but I didn't say anything. After the rehearsal, we got the suits out of our cases and smoothed the creases, left them hanging in the dressing room and went to go to the hotel.

Outside the stage door were a group of six or seven teenage girls, one of them squealed when she saw me. 'Here he is!' I turned round expecting to see B.B. but it was *my* autograph they wanted – *mine* and Jim's. I supposed they were there every day and didn't think much about it. Jim and I went off laughing with a couple of the girls following us right to the hotel which was about a quarter of a mile away.

A porter showed us to our rooms on the second floor, he asked us both for our autographs. The girl at the reception had given me a small card with the room number and price on it. I noticed the cost of the room for one night was half of what I earned for a full week's work as a milkman.

We spent the afternoon wandering round the town looking in shop windows and after that, we strolled through the dock area. Jim was pointing out what different flags meant on different ships. He was enjoying this. Apart from a summer holiday at Portsmouth ten years ago he hadn't been near the sea, it was all coming back to him now. He told me some stories of the times when he was a matelot and had me enthralled. I realised why he could put so much into the songs he had written – he was a very worldly person, drawing on a lifetime of experience.

Before we knew it, we had to rush to get to the theatre, the time had flown. We grabbed a cup of tea and a sand-

73

wich at some small café, and made it by bus with half an hour to spare.

Solly was waiting in the dressing-room.

'Come on, lads!' he gasped. 'You're s'posed to be here an hour before the show begins – that's a rule of the theatre.'

'Why an hour?' I asked.

'To get dressed and get your make-up on.'

'Make-up? What make-up?'

'Look, Harry boy ...' He was doing his Alf Garnett again. '... if you go out on that stage without make-up, you're going to look like a white sheet when those big spotlights hit you.'

I hadn't thought about buying make-up, neither had Jim.

'Haven't you got any?' Sol asked, before we could reply he had dived out of the room to ask one of the girls who did a routine with Billy Bassett to lend us some powder and mascara.

He must have told the girl we knew nothing about make-up and she offered to help.

She came in all smiles, in a flimsy wrap-over that did nothing to hide her massive boobs.

She had a great sense of humour and took over right away.

'Sit down,' she said, pushing me onto a chair facing the mirror – she picked a towel up from the wash basin, put it round my neck and said: 'Right, sir! Short back and sides?'

She produced a stick of dark brown make-up and proceeded to spread it on my face.

'Watch how I'm doing this because you'll have to do it yourself tomorrow – I'm not a bleedin' wet nurse,' she joked.

She spat in a little black box that contained mascara and put it on my eyes – she murmured – 'Some people have

74

all the bleedin' luck, look at the length of these eye-lashes – me! I have to buy mine.'

Her name was Beryl Baker and I liked her from that moment – she seemed to speak our language. After she had put the make-up on both Jim and me, she went, telling us if there was anything she could do for us just to come up to her dressing-room, any shorts that needed buttons or anything ironed, or, if we fancied a cup of tea it would always be ready. Then she said as an afterthought: 'Oh – be careful of B.B. – don't let all that charm fool you!' Then she was gone.

The Tannoy system told us the show had started – we dressed and admired ourselves in the full-length mirror. Jim had a ruffled white shirt that for some reason kept reminding me of when I was an altar boy. He looked good in his, I wasn't so sure of myself. I think I looked too stiff and formal, it wasn't the gear a fellow sits on a stool in, the trousers were flared but tight round the thighs, they weren't made for sitting in.

A voice over the Tannoy told us we would be 'on' in five minutes – now the excitement was beginning to rise in me. We walked down to the stage and stood in the wings.

'You follow this act,' whispered the stage manager.

We could see through the curtains a magician producing birds from handkerchiefs, he was getting good applause. For his finale, he showed the audience a bloody great chicken that squawked and clucked above the music. The curtains came across and as he was taking a bow in front of them, several stage hands rushed on, cleared his props, set up a chair for Jim and a high bar stool for me, then we were ushered on. Just as we sat down the orchestra played our music – the curtains opened to show rows and rows of people applauding, applauding *us*.

I had been given a hand mike and was sitting there holding it – the applause deadened Jim's guitar introduction which he had started to play immediately the curtains had opened, neither had the orchestra heard him – Jim realised what had happened and began the introduction to 'Spanish Eyes' again.

I sang it through and as I finished the last note, the stage electrician brought the lights up until we could not see beyond the first two rows. There was loud applause and shouts of 'More!' here and there.

Jim had learned his lesson from the awkward start we had made and did not begin the introduction until there was dead silence – it was a good effect. We made a clean start to 'You Only Have to Smile' and received what I had learnt was a 'big hand'.

At the finish of our act, there were people, not many, but one here and there, standing up applauding.

The curtains closed and the interval was announced, as I walked off the stage with Jim, B.B. was in the wings, he had been watching us perform and was most complimentary.

'Very nice – very nice indeed – I'll see you two are on with me more often.' He said this quite loudly.

'You're in,' winked the stage manager.

We went to our dressing-room where Solly was wide-eyed with excitement.

'Get those suits off,' he ordered. 'Don't get them creased – hang them up.'

We both got out of them immediately.

'How were we?' I asked.

'How were you? Didn't you hear those hands being put together? They weren't doing that to keep warm, my boys – they loved you.'

'B.B. liked us,' said Jim.

'Listen ...' said Solly in a whisper meant only for the three of us, '... in a few months' time, you two could be employing *him*.'

76

Solly was serious, he believed in us that much.

'He asked if you could go to Glasgow with him next week.'

'What did you say?' It was Jim asking.

'I told him if he upped the money to cover the fares and hotels, we'd go!'

'What did he say then?'

'He said yes – you know why? Because he knows a good act when he sees it.'

I looked at my wristwatch, it was nine-fifteen – our act had lasted nine minutes – it was hard to believe we had walked round Bristol for most of the day waiting to do that nine minutes.

'What happens now, Solly?'

'We'll go and have a look at Billy Bassett in the second half then go back to the hotel and have some supper.'

We washed off the make-up that Beryl had put on us and walked down to the stage – there were gales of laughter coming from the auditorium, and the laughter was for Billy Bassett who was telling 'camp' jokes mostly about him being followed by sailors in Bristol. He knew the names of most of the local pubs, the streets where the prostitutes are supposed to trade, he knew all the outlying districts and made it sound as if he was doing the act especially for the Bristol people – they lapped it up too. You had to admire him, his timing was perfect. His big eyes would hold a woman helpless with laughter in the front row, at the right moment he said: 'Careful love – somebody else has got to sit in that seat!'

I had never really cared for him before but I realised why he was a bill topper. He certainly knew how to make people laugh.

On walked Beryl, she had built her 'knockers' up. They looked as if they measured fifty-four inches or more. When

Billy got an eyeful of these, he just stood there frozen with his eyes popping.

'I've heard of Bristol Cities ...' he said. The audience fell about.

'I've got a great idea what you can put between those.'

'What?' said Beryl innocently.

'The Bristol Suspension Bridge.'

He went on like this for another half an hour, he finished to loud applause.

He brushed past us to his dressing-room and we left for the hotel. By now I was really hungry.

As we came out of the stage door, we were seen by a few of the patrons, they felt in their bags for programmes and we were asked to autograph them – suddenly, we had about a hundred people all wanting us to sign programmes, bits of paper, cigarette packets – anything.

Solly had ordered three cold suppers. We walked into the deserted restaurant, the night porter had put one of the lights on in the corner where two tables had some cold meats, salad, a jar of mayonnaise and some jelly with fruit embedded in it.

'Can we have a pot of tea for three?' asked Solly.

The porter mumbled something about not being able to leave the desk but he'd do his best when he got time.

We watched him slouch out, then the three of us began talking at once.

'It seemed to be over so quickly,' I said.

'How long were we on for?' Jim asked Solly.

'You did nine minutes – but I think you ought to work on two or three more numbers, then put them in.'

We talked eagerly for several minutes – suddenly, the doors opened as if by themselves and in breezed B.B., he had his manager and some young kid who we later found was his dresser, valet, driver and maid-of-all-work.

'Ooh,' he said eyeing us. 'I see the gannets are seated.'

Solly laughed dutifully.

'The manager liked you – so did the audience by the sound over the speaker – you went well – don't go too well though, otherwise I'll have to get rid of you.'

All this B.B. said as he removed his coat and began to pile meat and salad on his plate.

The doors opened again and in came the night porter, the slouch had gone, he was beaming a loving smile at Billy Bassett.

'Everything all right, Mr Bassett?' he asked.

'It looks all right Edward – are you all right?'

The porter nodded.

'Wife keeping well, Edward?'

'She had a twinge last winter – you remember last time you were here she was having that short-windedness – always puffed out she was – remember?'

'I remember,' said B.B.

'Well, she's over that!'

'Good! Now you go and get short of breath by bringing two nice chilled bottles of Chablis.'

The old porter said: 'Right away, Mr Bassett,' he went away chuckling. As the doors closed on him B.B.'s smile vanished and he muttered: 'Silly old bastard!'

Solly gave one of his loud laughs and started to butter up B.B.

'I think you're the greatest thing in this country today – you had that audience eating out of your hand.'

'Thank you, Mr-er ...' B.B. snapped his fingers.

'Segal – Solomon Segal – Solly.' Solly got up from our table and walked over to B.B. fishing for and producing a business card.

'I wish I was lucky enough to handle you, Mr Bassett – you're what I *call* a star!'

'Thank you, dear man – perhaps one day – who knows.'

'You never know,' said Solly.

It was apparent that B.B. could take all the flattery Solly was willing to give.

As Solly returned to our table, he said again, loud enough for B.B. to hear: 'What a star!'

We both nodded, I couldn't help thinking we were just as big crawlers as he was.

The porter returned with the wine and after removing the corks, B.B. told him to fill our glasses too, we toasted him with loud 'Cheers!' and he replied with 'Saludi'.

He sent for two more bottles and suggested that instead of us all shouting across at each other, we go and sit at his table.

'You sit here,' said B.B. to me. He pushed the dresser out of the chair and offered the empty seat to me.

'Tell me about yourself, darling,' he squeezed my thigh. 'What did you do before you became a – er – singer?'

'I was a milkman.'

'Were you?'

'So was he,' I said nodding to Jim.

'I'm not interested in him – I'm interested in you.' He murmured this, the wine had made him quite sloppy looking. 'Did you ever play any naughty games when you were a milkman?' The rest sat round with half smiles on their faces pretending not to listen.

Jim broke the silence: 'Come on, son – you've had a long day.' He rose and looked at me to follow.

'Are you his nurse?' asked B.B.

'No, Mr Bassett but we've been up since early this morning, we ought to be in the sack by now.'

I could see that B.B. had taken a dislike to Jim for breaking up the party, so I came to his defence.

'Jim's right, Billy, I'm dead beat, we ought to be in bed.'

'Billy? Don't you mean Mr Bassett?' he sulked.

'I'm sorry,' I said, 'It's just ... that ...'

80

Solly had jumped up laughing his over-amplified laugh. 'It's just that nobody ever thinks of you as Mister – you're such a well known face, it doesn't occur to any of us to call you Mister ... you're good old Billy.'

He laughed again. B.B.'s answer was a weak smile.

'Good night Mr Bassett!' said Sol.

'Call me Billy,' said B.B. Then winked.

9

B.B. ordered another bottle of wine, then asked his manager and dresser to leave him. He sat there sipping the liquor slowly and gazing at the chair Harry Selfridge had been sitting in. He rubbed his hand across the plastic seat that was still warm and found it gave him a strange sensation.

He drank the wine to the dregs and slowly eased himself up from the table, it was now well after midnight, the foyer was empty. The porter was reading an evening paper which he folded as B.B. emerged from the dining-room.

'Are you all right, Mr Bassett?'

'Yes, thank you Edward!' he slurred.

'Would you like your key, Mr Bassett?'

'What a good man you are.' Bassett had that stage smile on.

Edward preened at the compliment.

'We've got to look after you, Mr Bassett – they're only a few of you left.'

He passed the key to B.B. He took it, made towards the lift and as an afterthought said:

'By the way, Edward – which room is Mr Selfridge in?'

The porter consulted a large book.

'Two eighteen – same floor as you, sir.'

'He asked me to give him a couple of aspirins – I – er – don't want to – er – wake him up if he's – asleep – Have you – er – got a spare key to two eighteen, Edward?'

'Of course I have, anything for you Mr Bassett.' He rummaged around in a large drawer, then pulled out a key with an enormous tab with 218 embossed on it.

'Thank you, Edward.' He pocketed the key and walked into the lift.

'Goodnight Edward!'

When he got to his room, he undressed slowly, put on some fresh silk pyjamas, a silk dressing gown, and stepped into some black leather slippers. On a table in front of him was the key to 218. His eyes were glued to it.

He walked to a cabinet, took out a new bottle of brandy and poured half a glass. As he sipped from the glass, he reminded himself that what he was planning to do was all wrong, it had been a near thing two or three times already. As he drank his second glass, he reasoned he could not get in trouble by going to see a young man he could give some advice to. To hell with it!

He put his own key and the key to 218 in his pocket, opened the door and crept gently down the corridor. He tapped quietly on the door of 218, not loud but loud enough for the occupant to hear. There was no reply. He tapped again and waited – again, no reply. He put the key in the lock and turned it slowly. Harry Selfridge had left a small table light on, by this B.B. could see him sleeping like a child – he was naked with just a sheet half-covering him.

B.B. sat and gazed at him breathing shallowly. He bent forward and gently kissed the naked shoulder, he had an overwhelming desire to kiss him all over but didn't. He kissed his chest and as he did the sleeping figure stirred.

It seemed as if I had been asleep for only ten minutes or so when I began thinking of when I worked at the brewery, it came back to me vividly – I was dreaming of those wooden casks that had the smell of beer, hours after they had been put over the steam jets or hosed out. The fumes made me want to cough, I felt I was choking, I began to splutter. I woke up and sitting on the side of my bed was

Billy Bassett – he had brandy fumes coming from him, that's what I could smell.

'There – there – there,' he was saying.

'What are you doing?' I gasped.

'I was passing your room and I heard you choking, I came to see if I could get you anything.'

I was wide awake now.

'How did you get in?'

'Your door was open – you don't think I'd come in if I thought you were all right – I thought you were having a fit.'

'No – I'm fine.'

'Well you might thank me – I went downstairs to place a call and heard you, you are all right, aren't you?'

'Yes-er yes thanks, Mr Bassett.'

'We're not going to start again are we Harry – it's Billy – I'm Billy – your friend.'

As he said 'your friend', he put his hand on my knees. I just lay there, like that joke they tell about 'not knowing which way to turn'.

I started to weigh him up, he was not quite as tall as me but he was deceptively strong and fit, if he started anything I was going to need all the cunning I could find to come off best.

'You're going to be a big star, Harry,' he was rubbing my knees the way those lady masseurs do.

'Am I, Billy?' I grinned.

'I promise you – you've got all the ingredients Harry – looks, youth, nice voice – you've got it all going for you – nothing can stop you – some expert advice – I can give you that – I'll give you all the advice you want.'

I said: 'Thanks, Billy,' which I shouldn't have done because there and then he decided I wanted his advice.

'Move over,' he said, he undid his dressing gown, which he let fall to the floor.

'Might as well be comfy.'

He got in beside me. It was a double bed so I could hardly do anything else but 'move over'.

'Journalists and sociologists have been trying to define what star quality is for years. I've got it – you've got it – they waste time and energy filling up their papers trying to decide what people like us have to make mass audiences behave the way they do ...'

He had, by now, put his hands under the sheet and was groping my thighs again, much harder now, he turned to smile that smile he kept for warming his audience, his breath came like a four ale bar that hadn't been swept for a month.

'... let me kiss you, Harry,' he pleaded.

'Pardon?' I said.

B.B. put both his massive arms around me and began biting my neck.

'Hey, cut it out – Mr Bassett,' I pleaded.

'Billy – call me Billy – beautiful Harry!' He sounded like a tube train door opening.

'Christ,' I thought – 'if this is show business – tonight is my farewell appearance!' I tried to fight him off.

He got on top of me, he seemed as strong as a brewer's dray. Suddenly, I turned to see Jim Lloyd standing in the doorway. He just had a pair of boxer shorts on.

'You two enjoying yourselves?' he asked sarcastically.

'Out!' said Jim to B.B. He stood aside to let B.B. pass. 'Don't ever let me catch you with him again!' Jim shouted 'Out,' again.

B.B. looked like he was going to argue but the sight of Jim standing there like a light heavyweight made him think better of it. He picked up his dressing gown, felt in the pocket for his door key and mumbled something about, '... just a bit of fun.'

Jim closed the door and stood looking quietly at me.

'You're not bent, are you?' he asked seriously.

' 'Course I'm not bloody bent – he's bloody bent not *me* – I woke up to find him sitting on my bed.'

I told Jim the full story of how I had found him there.

'You'd better lock your door in future, son.' He sat down beside me. 'I heard voices – I'm in the room next door – I was lying there thinking about us.'

'What do you mean, Jim?'

'Harry, I don't think I'm cut out for this life.'

Eileen Dutton sat at her office desk. Things were not going right. Two of her best delivery men were away 'having a go' at show business, two others were off, one with heart trouble, the other on holiday.

Some of the other fellows had helped out by delivering on Harry Selfridge's and Jim Lloyd's rounds but she knew this could not go on indefinitely, she also wondered if, after tasting the life of show business, they could both settle down as milk roundsmen again.

It was important to keep her old customers. She wished she was a man, at least she could get on a float and ride the crisis, she knew all about deliveries, perhaps she might do that, it would be a nice change, the paperwork was making her head buzz. She also felt she owed it to her father to make a success of Dutton's. It didn't seem right to see forty-odd years of hard work go overboard because of her incompetence. She was going to *make* it work.

By Friday, we were enjoying ourselves. The audiences had been great, they had cheered each performance, we had added one more song and with a few pointers from different people, we had added a little polish to our act in only a few evenings.

On the morning after the incident in the hotel, there

was a tap on our dressing-room door, I opened it to see B.B. standing there. His head was hanging and he whispered: 'May I come in?' There was just Jim and myself in the room, Solly was 'phoning somebody in London from the call box in the stage doorkeeper's office. I stood aside to let him pass.

'Sure, come in,' I said.

'I've come to apologise,' he said to the linoleum.

We both stood awkwardly. Jim spoke. 'Don't worry Mr Bassett – we've forgotten it – haven't we, Harry?' I nodded.

'It was stupid of me. I'm not trying to whitewash myself but touring is a very lonely business – I drank too much last night – my reasoning went and I feel ashamed of my behaviour – especially to yourselves who have only been in our profession for five minutes.'

Jim spoke again: 'Look, Mr Bassett – it takes all sorts to make a world – some of us are not made like others – we all have our faults. It has taken a lot of guts to come in here and apologise the way you are doing and for that we are grateful – as far as we are concerned, it never happened – we have forgotten it.' He held out his hand. B.B. looked up from the floor and took it slowly, if it had been one of those American films the music would have swelled – the camera would have pulled back and celestial voices from an all-girl choir would have been going full blast.

I shook his hand. B.B. clasped it with both hands whispering: 'Thank you – thank you.' Then he was gone. It was quiet again, a full minute went by.

'This lark is full of surprises, isn't it?' I said.

'It sure is – I meant what I said, though – he had to find a lot of guts to come in here and do that. He is top of the bill and we are nothing – I have got a lot more

respect for Billy Bassett than I had this time yesterday.'
Jim was very impressed.

On Friday we were like kids at school on visiting day.
Daphne and the kids were coming down from London.
They were arriving by train and we were to meet them at
the station. We stood at the barrier waiting for them to
appear, commuters were giving us wide smiles as they
hurried from the train. Quite a few recognised us, suddenly above the bobbing heads, I saw Daphne and
company.

'There she is, Jim!'

They saw us and broke into a run, a few seconds later
we were all embracing each other. Daphne had big tears
welling up, she kept dabbing her eyes with a crumpled
handkerchief.

'What are you crying for?' laughed Jim.

'I love you,' said Daphne unashamed.

'I love you, too – but I'm not flooding the platform,
am I?'

'I haven't seen you for a week – don't I get a kiss?'

Jim grabbed her, then kissed her neck, her ears, her
eyes, her lips, the kids hung on to his legs.

Above all this I heard a piercing scream.

'Yoo-hoo! Harry boy!' I turned to see a blonde in a
yellow outfit with shoes and handbag to match wobbling
down the platform on four-inch high soles. It was my old
lady.

'Yoo-hoo! Harreee-!' She was holding Benjy's arm.
'It's me – mummy!'

She rushed up, grabbed me by the ears and planted
lipstick all over me. 'How's my little boy?' she asked.
Benjy was pumping my hand. 'Hello star,' he said.

I must say my mother looked good, she had worked on
her appearance. Hair-do, manicure – she had a good per-
fume on and looked fifteen years younger, she could have

made it with any thirty-year-old fellow and he'd never have known her age.

'Ma, you look great,' I said.

'Ooh, ta.' She patted her hair either side. 'When you've got a star for a son you've got to look the part.' She took my arm and led me towards the exit. They had arrived on the five-fifteen so we went to the hotel. We organised some tea and cakes, they were all impressed with the décor and uniforms of the staff as they stuffed the cucumber sandwiches. We showed them our rooms, they couldn't get over the fact we had our own bathrooms – one each.

At eight o'clock we left for the Empire. We managed to get two extra seats for the old lady and Benjy. The show had been sold out well in advance but Solly talked the manager into letting us have two of the house seats.

As soon as the curtain opened on our act, I could see the bright yellow outfit in the fourth row, the audience applauded but the old lady's hands were still going when the rest had stopped. I heard her say, 'Good old Harry!'

At the end of our first song, she was whooping it up – sticking her fingers in her mouth whistling and shouting, 'More! More!' She was actually getting the rest of the audience at it too – there were loud cries of 'More!' and 'Encore!' from the rest. It didn't go un-noticed by Solly.

The visitors proudly stood back as we signed dozens of autographs outside the stage door after the show. I heard the old lady whisper to several people: 'He's my son!' To say she stood there like a peahen would be an understatement, she was telling each of them how she had brought me up and how she knew I always had it in me. Benjy backed her up in everything. 'You his father?' asked one customer. 'Sort of,' I heard Benjy reply.

We hadn't thought of asking them to stay overnight,

suddenly we had to rush for the last train to London. We made it with only thirty seconds to spare. As the train pulled out, I turned to see Jim crying.

10

Next day at lunch what I had feared happened. Solly was busy telling us our movements for the following week at Glasgow. Jim was stirring his coffee, not taking any notice of the proceedings, he wasn't the least bit excited to hear that our single record had just entered the Top Ten.

Solly became aware of his lack of enthusiasm. 'You feel all right, Jim?' he asked.

'Yes, I'm fine.' He didn't look up from his coffee stirring.

'You don't seem to be with it,' said Solly.

Jim cleared his throat and began to speak quietly. 'I told Harry a few days ago that I don't think I'm cut out for this life...'

Solly was about to bluster out: 'What do you mean?' But Jim stopped him.

'... hear me out, please Solly. Harry is a young fellow, the kids love him, he looks good – he sings well – it's what the punters want to hear. He is unique, there's no other Harry Selfridge, he doesn't model himself on anybody, he is an original. Me, on the other hand, there's a couple of thousand of us in this town alone, I am a guitarist, a tiny bit above average. If I became ill tomorrow, you could find fifty people to do my job and glad of it. I'm coming up for the half hundred and a fifty-year-old guitarist backing Harry is going to hinder him, not help him...'

We both listened as he continued.

'... it may sound strange but I enjoyed myself delivering those bottles of milk, going home to my kids, painting the house now and again ... coming home finding Daphne there ... sleeping in my own bed with the woman ... I er ... well ... I love.'

'What are you trying to say?' asked Solly.

'I think I would like Harry to make his own way ... he is capable ... you are a good manager Solly, you can help him far more than I can ... I will come to Glasgow if you want me to next week, but ... after that I'd like to return to the life I know ... this has been a good interlude ... I wouldn't have missed it for the world but I'd rather go back to London.'

There was a long silence, we knew that Jim meant every word he was saying.

Solly asked, 'What about the fortune waiting for you?'

Jim grinned, 'I'll manage.'

That was when Jim really left the act. The following week in Glasgow, Solly brought up a young fellow from London whom he introduced as Catgut Lowery, he was supposed to be a great musician, one of the best in the land. He played an acoustic guitar and was also a fine arranger. He was about thirty with rimless glasses and hair that was a bit too long. He had an amused look in his eyes that never left them. When Jim heard him play, he couldn't believe it, Catgut's hands flew up and down the fretboard of the guitar, the long bony fingers plucked music that sounded like a full orchestra.

Jim gasped, 'Wow!' as he finished. 'I'm going to burn my guitar – you've made me feel really inadequate!'

We rehearsed for the rest of the week with Catgut taking Jim's place for the Saturday night performance. I hated to admit it, but Jim's absence made not one bit of difference to the ovation I got. Maybe it was those Glaswegians who seemed to be less inhibited than us Southerners but they cheered me as if I was Dylan or Tom Jones or somebody.

After the show, we all caught the sleeper back to London. Jim was the happiest man in Glasgow as he stepped aboard the express leaving for King's Cross.

As we chugged out of Central Station, I wondered what it was going to be like without him. I walked down the corridor to the loo. Catgut was just coming out. The toilet was filled with blue smoke. I vaguely recognised the smell – Catgut was on marijuana.

I got off the sleeper at seven-thirty, there were plenty of taxis outside the station. I gave the driver our address in Battersea, Solly promised to call me if there was anything to report. Jim had got a cab after a quick, 'I'll call you,' over his shoulder.

Catgut was still sleeping in his bunk on the train. As the cab cut across the West End, I wondered what I was going to do. Solly had asked me not to go back to work because he was sure it would only be a matter of days before offers came in.

We passed two or three milk floats, I got a great urge to have a look at Dutton's. I gave the driver new instructions, to take me to Dutton's. I only had one case which wasn't heavy. There might be somebody there I could have a chat with.

I paid the taxi driver – from what he charged me I could have bought a bloody taxi of my own. The cab roared off, I stood gazing through the gates into the yard.

I must have stood there three or four minutes when a Mini pulled up. Out of it got Eileen Dutton, my apple-tart started pounding away again.

'Hello, Harry,' she said, all surprised. She was in jeans, a white sweat shirt that had a big strawberry on it, soft shoes and no make up, she looked good enough to eat.

'Hello, Miss Dutton.'

'What are you doing here?'

'I was on my way home – I've just come from Scotland.'

'How was it up there, Harry?'

'All right.'

'Did they like you?'

'Well, they let me live!'

'I've come to get some forms I forgot – have you had breakfast?'

'No, not yet – I was just going home...'

Before I could finish, she took my arm: 'Come on – we'll have some eggs and bacon'. She fumbled for some keys and unlocked the gate, then led me up the yard towards the office. She rummaged around in the fridge, produced tomato juice, then eggs and bacon as if by magic. In six minutes flat, I had hot bacon and eggs, toast and marmalade with a half of pint of full cream to wash it down.

'How is it, Harry?'

'Fine thanks, Miss.' She smiled every time I said 'Miss'. She seemed to like it.

'You eat like you haven't had a meal for a month.'

I suddenly realised I hadn't eaten since yesterday lunchtime, there had been no time to get anything before we boarded the train in Glasgow. I told her I hadn't had anything for almost twenty hours.

'Why not?' She was most concerned.

'Well, y'know, theatrical people don't usually eat before shows, and we were in a rush to pack and catch the train...'

'Let me tell you something, Harry Selfridge – star of TV stage and radio – half the people with ulcers and tummy trouble have it because they missed meals, their stomachs weren't lined, they deteriorated ... and ...' She gave a shrug. 'Have another slice of bacon.' She watched me devour it and said: 'Did you really enjoy it?'

'I really did.'

'Harry – I can't see you coming back here to work but if you ever want to, you know you always can – that's if we're still here!'

'What do you mean, Miss?'

This time she didn't smile. 'We're going into the red.' She flicked an envelope from the bank – 'These people are pressing for the overdraft.'

I didn't know too much about overdrafts but it was obvious it was something she didn't want.

'Two thousand pounds is a lot of money when you haven't got it.'

'Two pounds is a lot when you haven't got it,' I said.

'You're right, Harry.' She began to clear up. In the middle of it she stopped. 'Are you still going to take me up the river?'

'Sure,' I said.

'When?'

'Any time.'

'Today?'

'If you like.'

'See you back here at midday?'

'Right.'

'Right – I'll be here.'

I rushed out, picking up my case as I went. 'See you at twelve!'

I have savoured days I have enjoyed. I can remember a few. A trip to Margate as a kid when I dug a sandcastle as big as the roundabout in the kids' park, I can remember watching from the prom as the tide came in and crumbled the turrets I had made with my bucket and spade.

I remembered when I had got a school prize, a first for English and composition, no names were announced until

95

the actual prize giving. I was twelve, the prize was a book of poems by Walter de la Mare, I took it home and read half of it. When I got home next day, I couldn't find it.

'Where's my book?' I asked the old lady.

'Book? What book?'

'A book of poems.'

'Oh that.' She got up and went into the loo – she came out with it.

'This it?'

I opened it to find several of the flimsy pages missing.

'We ran short of paper,' she said.

That book was my most prized possession. I couldn't find any words to say when she handed it to me minus the pages, I just cried.

Those days and a few others stayed in my mind. The day on the river will stay with me for all time.

We met at midday. She drove me to the pier at Westminster, parked the car on a meter, it was Sunday so she didn't have to worry about the time. We paid our money and boarded the boat going to Hampton Court. The day had been overcast at first but now it had turned into a hot summery afternoon. She was still in her jeans and T-shirt but had added make-up.

We pulled away from the pier going up river towards Kew and Richmond. The fellow with the microphone gave us a commentary on buildings north and south of the Thames, from the Houses of Parliament up to the new Covent Garden – then Putney, Hammersmith, Richmond. We saw the bridges from water level, I saw the houses I served as a milkman, I was able to tell Miss Dutton who bought milk – who had butter, who had cheese, yoghurts, she was in fits of laughter at my descriptions.

'You ought to be a comedian – not a singer, Harry.' She felt for my hand and squeezed it. 'I'm glad you were there today – I needed cheering up.'

'I'm glad *you* were there – I was hungry.'
She laughed again and kissed me on the cheek.
There was no doubt about it, Yours Truly was in love.

11

In just over three weeks, lots of things had happened. 'You only have to smile' had gone to the number one spot in the Hit Parade.

Solly had signed a five year contract with Lantern Records and under its terms I was to make at least two albums a year. I was to get nine per cent of the sales, rising the following year to ten per cent, then eleven and so on until the final year when it would stay at twelve per cent.

Lantern Records had advanced Solly five thousand pounds against royalties, that meant that when our royalty cheque was paid it would be less the five thousand. After paying commission to Solly, Jim and I split the rest, Jim also had a large amount to come as composer of the song.

The record had been released in America and seemed to be doing well, they told us it was expected to 'break' in a few weeks.

Solly had moved into some nicer offices in Bond Street and he'd also got himself a secretary.

I had moved from Battersea into a block of flats just up near Marble Arch. I had a woman coming in every other day to clean, she was named Ethel, nice sort, tidied up, washed up and laundered any linen that looked soiled. Solly had made arrangements to pay her, pay the rent and rates and any expenses I had. All I had to do was to keep working to ensure the money was coming in to pay for all this newly-acquired luxury.

I was booked on a run of one-night stands, we were sold out at each one. I guested on three major television shows.

The fans were getting rougher, at the end of the performances, they rushed the stage screaming: 'Harry – Harry!' At first I enjoyed it, but outside the stage doors they turned into little sods, their average age was only fifteen but as I was trying to sign my name on a programme or piece of paper, some randy little git would be groping me.

After a week or so of this, Solly arranged for me to be sneaked out of a side door into a waiting car.

Two weeks later every newspaper had pictures of me, in action, stripped to the waist, in bathing trunks. In women's magazines, I wrote about my favourite recipe – if they only knew – I could just about make tea and toast. One was going on about Lobster Thermidor – I'd had it once and enjoyed it – I supposed they picked that because the lobster looked good in a colour magazine.

'You only have to smile' entered the Hit Parade in America. Solly had suggested I go to New York to plug it. He had arranged with somebody over there for me to appear on shows like the Merv Griffith Show and the Johnny Carson Show, plus quite a lot of radio shows.

I was really excited about this, I had never been in an aeroplane. The idea of flying to New York got me so excited I wanted to be ill.

We left on a Sunday from Heathrow. We had travelled by coach from Victoria, Solly said it was the best way to go. As we stepped off the coach at the air terminal, a scream went up from thousands of teenage throats.

I turned to see four policemen coming towards me to 'protect' me. Up on the roof, there were banners and placards being waved, on them was written 'Come back soon Harry!' and 'We love you Harry!' Some of those kids were actually crying with ecstasy. I waved to them and the screams doubled in volume.

The policemen pushed back any kids that tried to get

near me and led me to the V.I.P. room to await the call to board the aeroplane.

Most of the other passengers were American, they gave me no more than a casual glance. Solly was all smiles, 'You'll be the biggest thing since the Beatles.' He rubbed his hands like he was kneading dough. 'If you click with this record in the States, I don't think you or I will have to worry financially for the rest of our days.' I watched him savour the idea and said: 'What would I make from a number one hit in the States?' He smiled and thought for a moment, 'With radio stations paying royalties, plus sales, I would say – a hundred-thousand dollars.'

I looked at him quite seriously and said: 'Solly – can you do me a favour?'

'Anything Harry.'

'Lend me ten pence, I want to buy the *News of the World*.'

This was another day that will linger in my memory. The smiling hostesses, the seat belts, the take off, the meals on trays, the view from the air as we rose 'up, up and away'. The people like ants on the ground – the cars looking like Dinky toys, the white fluffy clouds and suddenly blue glorious sky with a sun clearer than I have ever seen.

The captain sent his regards and asked if I would like to go on the flight deck. Wow! I had never been so thrilled, it looked out of space in that cockpit. Later I watched a film starring Sean Connery. I signed autographs for several of the crew and six hours later they told us to fasten our seat belts for landing at Kennedy Airport, New York.

Was it really happening? Christ, only weeks ago I was a milkman – now I was one of the jet set, I felt in my pocket for my sunglasses – if you're gonna be one of 'em – might as well look like 'em!

We passed through customs that had serious-faced men in denim shirts making checks with sheafs of papers. I had already been fingerprinted in London, when the customs clerk found my name, he smiled for the first time, then said: 'Have a good stay, Mr Selfridge.' A huge negro took our bags, placed them on a trolley and wheeled us to some waiting taxis, they were bright yellow, some were green and white, most of the drivers had sunglasses on and chewed gum, there was a grille between the driver and the passengers. I found out that this was to stop 'muggings' from 'muggers' who directed drivers to a quiet spot then held them up for their takings. We drove through the suburbs towards New York City, traffic was idling, most cars had children and older people in the back seats, like any Sunday in England really.

Then I saw the skyline of New York through the haze, first the United Nations building, the Empire State building, the river, I was to get to know this city well but that first glimpse made the most lasting of my memories, I could remember every traffic light, every stop until we arrived at the hotel on Seventh Avenue.

Things were very quiet as we drove through the streets, I guess because it was Sunday, it was something like the City of London, I could imagine the whole lot erupting the following day. We didn't even check into our rooms, as soon as we registered, I asked Solly to come for a walk.

We walked along 46th Street and came out onto Broadway, it was daylight but all the neon signs were on in Times Square, there were not a lot of people about, but every café, snack bar, record shop and souvenir shop was open. We just walked, stopping every few yards to look at the unbelievable height of the skyscrapers, the air seemed to have the smell of roasted peanuts in it, every other person was coloured, with small children who had candy floss or peanut brittle in their hands, stuffing it into their mouths.

It was coming up for evening. We realised we had been going for a long time because of the five hours difference, it was nearly eight o'clock but in fact it was one a.m. so we decided to go back to the hotel.

The rooms were all right. I didn't think they were too clean looking, not as nice as the ones in Bristol and Glasgow. Solly had all the dollars we had been allowed in London. He tipped the bell boys and staff, he felt good doing this until the waiter, whom he gave a dollar tip to, looked at it in disgust and said: 'Hell man, I don't own the joint!' He made Sol so uncomfortable he had to part with another dollar. As he slunk off, Solly said 'If he *doesn't* own the joint, he soon will!'

We slept like tops, the next thing I remember was Solly shaking me saying, 'Come on Harry, there's work to do!' It was a bright beautiful morning and I was about to be launched on the American public.

I had six days of running from radio stations to TV studios then to press interviews and was glad to return to London. I never thought that sort of life could be so exhausting. I was drained.

Frankie Farrell put down the paperback he was reading. Soon it would be lights out. It had been the same thing for well over three years. When the judge gave him five years for grievous bodily harm, he made up his mind that he would get it over as comfortably as he could. When he was released, he was never going to see the inside of a prison cell again.

No more was he going to spend months and months 'casing' a bank or warehouse, 'fixing' a gang to help him, organising routes and getaway cars to knock over a wages van or sub post-office, then find that at the end of it all he came out with five or six grand.

Banks didn't carry large sums these days, also those security vans made three, four, or sometimes five journeys to keep the sums down, it was wiser to take four loads of £25,000 rather than one load of £100,000. Even if you were successful, by the time you'd split with the others it was a wonder if you came out with £5,000. For five years inside, that worked out less than £20 a week and at today's prices that wouldn't even get you two sticks of gelignite.

Frankie turned on his bunk and figured out a few legitimate ways to spend the rest of his days in comfort. Days where he could do without a gang, do without violence and do without this rathole of a cell where he knew every crack, every indentation in the brickwork, knew the footsteps of every screw, knew the same faces and stories of every prisoner in the block.

He had pretty good horse sense, could add up as fast as any accountant, his job of looking after the prison library had given him a good insight into the literary world. He had memorised great speeches by Churchill, Hitler; the writings of Pepys and Johnson and could fool a lot of people with his knowledge, he could converse on almost any subject and had become chairman of the prison brains' trust.

He was pretty sure he would get paroled, maybe property development would be the game to enter. Most of the villains he knew were sitting pretty on renting out flats where the demand was greatest: Paddington, Brixton, Notting Hill. Maybe he would too, he only had a few months to go, he decided to wait until his release then sniff around a little.

The one thing he figured he had learned most about

was the behaviour of human beings. Every man has his price, every man has his breaking point, every man has his fears.

12

When we returned to London, Heathrow Airport looked like Wembley Stadium. The kids had got news we were on our way, this was all down to Solly who had wired our publicity man, Freddy Stacey. Freddy had begged us to return on a Saturday because that was the day he could cause the most chaos, also he could make the Sunday papers.

Holidaymakers and travellers were held up as the screaming fans tore through the lounges, they wore T-shirts emblazoned with 'Harry Selfridge' – 'Harry, the beautiful' – and 'I love Harry S'.

The screams that greeted me as I stepped onto the tarmac could be heard well above the noise of the taxying jets.

My record was now at Number One and the album I had made had been rushed out in advance and had beaten all previous sales in Lantern Records' history. I had pictures taken of myself being presented with a gold record by Miss World. Jimmy Savile interviewed me for a *'Top of the Pops'* show. There were the pop writers from every daily and ladies' magazines all gathered in the press room asking me questions that I answered with, 'yes' or 'no'.

They must have thought I was a bit of a berk because they started to phrase their own words and asked me for confirmation, so a journalist would say something like: 'I suppose the adulation you are witnessing today must make you feel grateful that these people have travelled all the way to London Airport to give you this tumultuous welcome, I suppose it must fill you with pride?'

I murmured: 'Er, yes.'

The next day I read that *I* had said to the waiting press:
'I am deeply grateful to those wonderful teenagers for
taking the time to welcome me back to my favourite city
and putting my record at Number One in the Hit Parade.'

The funny thing was, I honestly believed *I* said that.
Freddy Stacey was doing a great job promoting Harry
Selfridge.

I 'phoned Jimmy Lloyd as soon as I got to the safety
of the flat.

'Hello Jimmy, how's things?'

'Where are you, Harry?'

'I'm in London – at the flat – just got back from New
York – what are you doing?'

'I'm sitting here watching sport on television.'

'I've got a lot to tell you.'

'Why don't you come over – you could be here in
twenty minutes if you get a taxi – you *can* afford a taxi,
can't you?'

'I'll get washed and shaved and be there by five.'

'I'll have a cup of tea ready. Cheers Harry!'

'Cheers Jim!'

Daphne had the kettle going full blast as I signed the taxi
driver's autograph book outside Jim's house in Meadow
Road.

Since I had last been there, Jim had had the place re-
decorated, new furniture, a hi-fi system wired up in quadro-
phonic. He had my album on the turntable as I walked
in, the kids hugged me, Daphne wrapped her cuddly frame
round me saying: 'Hello gorgeous'. Jim held my hand
looking into my eyes, if I could think of another word
I'd use it but I can't ... as he looked at me it was ... love.
Not that queer sort of love, it was love for a fellow man
who just enjoyed seeing his mate do well.

'Turn that down,' I said pointing to the record player, 'I can't stand that fellow!' They all laughed and Jim switched me off.

We talked for two hours. I told them about New York. The streets, the people, the TV, the disc jockeys, the record scene, the hotels, the girls, the men, the theatres, I felt like that fellow in the painting of Raleigh's Boyhood.

Jim told me that things were looking bad at the dairy. Eileen could not go on much longer, she needed a loan that the bank were reluctant to give, if it wasn't forthcoming, she most certainly would have to let every worker go. Jim was sitting pretty, he had had several cheques from the recording company as composer of the Number One song in the country. He had about twenty thousand to come but had been warned that the tax would bite a large chunk out of it so he was playing it cagey before he got himself a new house and took the kids and Daphne off to Majorca for a holiday.

I told him I had to leave, what the hell for, I don't know. I was only going back to an empty flat but I pretended I had lots to do and left telling them all I'd see them soon.

Jim rang for a cab and I left, they all waved me off down the road, I sat in the back of the cab wondering what I was going to do on a Saturday night alone in London.

I looked at the digital watch Solly had given me as a present in New York, it was just after eight, I told the driver to take me to the Tavern, maybe I'd see a few of the lads there. I paid the driver off and noticed I had two quid left. I only had to ask Solly for money and he gave it readily but at that moment I had two quid – still it was enough for a drink or two. I pushed open the door of the saloon bar and went in. The bar was about three-quarters full. As I entered, the piano player suddenly stopped playing, the drummer gave a roll on the drums, somebody said: 'Harry Selfridge,' and applause broke out. I pushed my way through back-slappers towards the corner where Charlie Henderson, Ginger Smith and Johnny Dempsey were sure to be, and they were. 'Hello star', 'Hello money bags', 'Wotcher mate'. Before I could say hello, a big pint was shoved in my hand. 'Git it down you before the rush starts.'

I drank as fast as I could, as I emptied the glass another one was passed by Ginger Smith, 'Come on Harry, you've got a lot of catching up to do.' I sipped the white froth, it had been so long since I had a drink I was dizzy from the first pint, I would have to stall a bit.

Johnny Dempsey decided at that moment to go on shorts. I now stood with a pint in one hand and a double Scotch in the other, the company was in great mood ribbing me. I had to drink up, 'Cheers' I said as I downed the Scotch. Christ, it nearly knocked a hole in my chest. Halfway through the pint, Charlie Henderson said: 'Same again – your shout Harry!'

I suddenly realised I had two quid, I hoped I had enough for a round, just as I was about to call, in walked Johnny Mack and Albie Stevens.

'Make that six Scotches,' shouted Charlie, I fished in my pockets but all I could find was the two pounds and some small change.

'Three pounds fifty, please Harry,' the barman was looking at me all smiles as he separated the six Scotches neatly.

'I've only got two quid,' I said.

'What? What about all that bleedin' publicity we've been reading about you getting five grand a week?' said Charlie.

'I didn't put any more in my pocket.'

'We don't like Welshers do we?' said Johnny. It was in fun but I felt myself reddening up.

'No,' said Ginger Smith. 'There's enough bleedin' free-

108

loaders come in here without bleedin' pop stars coming it!'

They all laughed but there and then I made up my mind I would never let Solly give me pocket money again. In future I would never have less than a couple of hundred on me – I was going to start living like a star.

I made some feeble excuse about leaving and a promise to send Charlie the money he had paid to make the price of the drinks up. I got on a bus to Marble Arch with the change I had and walked into the empty flat. The fridge was empty, the flat was cold and Britain's number one record star was bloody miserable.

Frankie Farrell was out on parole. If he hadn't stopped to buy the Sunday papers it might have all been different. He opened them and found in each one pictures of a new pop star named Harry Selfridge.

He glanced at the pictures casually, he saw a good looking young fellow being protected by policemen as hundreds of teenyboppers pleaded with him to stop and talk. It was the heading made him look twice. 'Manager says Harry Selfridge is Britain's new superstar.' He read on. 'Solomon Segal, manager of Harry Selfridge said that the earning power of the pop singer could top the three million dollar mark during the coming year. Segal went on to say that Harry has had three firm offers for movies, the franchise from T-shirts, albums, photos etcetera, will put him into the earning bracket of the Beatles and Rolling Stones – the nice thing about Harry S is that he doesn't have to split four or five ways, Harry is solo ...'

Farrell read on, as he did a plan began to form in his criminal mind. The more he thought about it the more plausible it became.

He suddenly had a great desire to own a pop star. Yes, he liked the idea. He would also like to have a bit of

that three million dollars Solomon Segal had boasted abou
It must be better than thieving.

Solomon Segal arrived at his new office early Monday mo
ning. His secretary had put some carnations in a vase o
his desk, there were no messages but Solly felt confide
the 'phone would be ringing before long with intereste
bookers requiring Harry's services. He was on top of th
world.

The stories and pictures in yesterday's papers could hav
done Harry no harm, there were quite a few in Monday'
dailies that had managed to get a different angle on Harry'
arrival. Mostly dealing with the problem of teenybopper
that got crushed and had to go to hospital after Saturday'
scenes.

Solly smiled as the 'phone on his desk rang, 'Segal here
He had learned that bit in the States.

'My name is Frankie Farrell,' said the voice at th
other end.

'What can I do for you Mr Farrell?'

'I think it would be a good idea if you and I could hav
a talk.'

'A talk? What sort of a talk?'

'Mr Segal – it is impossible to talk over the 'phone
can you come to my hotel. I am at the Hilton in Par
Lane. It could mean a lot of money to you, probabl
more than you've ever dreamed of.'

Solly began to feel excitement creeping in.

'Is it about Harry Selfridge?'

'Right,' said Farrell.

'When can I come?'

'Come now if you like – I'm in the penthouse suite
the lift will bring you right up.'

'All right I'll be there in the next half hour.'

'Fine Mr Segal – I'll be waiting for you.'

Solly replaced the 'phone and sat gazing at the receiver. What would someone in the penthouse suite at the Hilton in Park Lane want with him on a Monday morning? There was only one way to find out – jump in a cab, go and see.

He instructed his secretary to take any messages but if anybody wanted him urgently he would be at the Hilton in Park Lane. He told her this as if it was an everyday occurrence, in fact he had never been in the Hilton in his life, he had never been able to afford even a snack there. He looked at his watch, it had just passed midday.

Frankie Farrell had booked the penthouse suite at the Hilton, the night before. He thought it a good address to sound out Solomon Segal. It had taken him only a few minutes to find out Segal's office and 'phone number but first he wanted to weigh up what sort of man he was. It seemed a good investment to rent a suite for the day, have flowers put in the room and a couple of bottles of Dom Perignon put on ice. So far he hadn't worked out any plan to move in on Harry Selfridge.

The 'phone rang, the porter said there was a Mr Segal at the desk to see him. Farrell thanked him and asked him to be shown up. He looked at his watch, it was twelve thirty-five.

A few minutes later a bell boy knocked at the door and announced, 'Mr Segal.'

Farrell had picked up the 'phone on hearing the knock on the door, as Solly entered he smiled and motioned to him to make himself at home. Farrell put his hand over the mouthpiece and said, 'Be with you in a moment Mr Segal.' Solly smiled and sat in the deep armchair Farrell had pointed to, he couldn't help overhearing the conversation. Farrell was shouting into the mouthpiece obviously talking to somebody overseas. 'Hello Jack! How are you?

111

How's the weather in LA? Listen Jack – I got your message about Pennsylvania Products – look – if they keep going up – buy! Watch them – if they go back more than five points – sell! We have to make at least fifty thousand – even if they lose five points. Huh? Yes that's my final word. Okay – keep in touch – let me know as soon as the market opens – 'Bye!'

He replaced the dead 'phone he had been talking to and walked smiling with hand outstretched towards Solly. 'Sorry about that, speaking to Los Angeles – Mr Segal?'

'Solomon Segal.' They shook hands.

'Can I get you a drink?' Before Solly could answer he had walked to the refrigerator and produced the champagne. 'There's only one drink at this time of day,' said Farrell as he eased the cork expertly. Solly watched the bubbles as he poured two glasses. 'To our meeting,' said Farrell.

'Oh cheers!' said Solly. He took two large gulps and liked the taste, his instinct told him he was drinking something good. 'What can I do for you Mr Farrell?'

'Frank – please Frankie – you are Solomon?'

'Solly, I'm known as.'

'Good Irish name,' said Farrell good-humouredly. 'Solly,' began Farrell. '...I don't want to waste your time because you must be a busy man – we are both busy men ...' He was now pacing the carpet as he sipped his champagne. '... Therefore I'll come to the point.' He refilled Solly's glass and began again. 'I am a wealthy man – most of my money has been made through property speculation ... I got out just before the slump and managed to hang on to all I made.

'I have several investments but there is no fun, no gamble, no excitement in what I'm doing – I would love to be on your side of the business, handling talent – watch it develop. How can I do it? How can I buy myself into

112

this world? I know very little about the entertainment game but seeing pictures in yesterday's paper of er what's his name – your singer ...' He snapped his fingers for Solly to enlighten him.

'Harry Selfridge?'

'That's him – Harry Selfridge – looks like a good talent – when I saw the pictures I thought people buy pieces of boxers and golfers what if I could invest something into a pop singer.' He filled Solly's glass, 'How can I do it?' He watched Solly sip the champagne and waited for him to speak.

'I don't know,' said Solly. 'It depends what you have in mind.'

Farrell pretended to think for a while then began pacing again.

'Look – money is cheap nowadays – the more you earn – the more the Government take – if a man in Britain today earns one million pounds in a year and he is honest – paying the tax the Chancellor demands – do you know how much he comes out with?'

Solly shook his head.

'Eleven thousand pounds! He actually keeps eleven grand.' He let this sink in. 'That means it takes him ten years to earn one hundred thousand pounds – right?'

'Right,' said Solly.

'Bearing what I've just said in mind ...' continued Farrell, '... how much would you consider taking in ready cash – no strings – just straight cash for a fifty per cent stake in your boy? Remember it's cash – it doesn't have to be declared – how much?'

Solly blinked, he had been taken right off his guard – the champagne had blunted the sharpness he prided himself on.

The training he'd had over the years as an agent suddenly came back to him. 'How much?' He ran his index finger

113

round the rim of the glass. 'It would have to be a lot.'

'Okay,' said Farrell, 'tell me!'

Solly didn't answer because he didn't know.

'Tell me,' said Farrell again. 'Five thousand – ten – twenty – what have you got in mind?'

Solly decided to chance his arm, 'I would want thirty thousand pounds.'

There was a silence. Farrell looked at the carpet and said, 'How much for the entire contract? How much for Harry Selfridge to join our organisation with no commitments to anybody else? One hundred per cent ours?'

Solly drank his champagne, then said, 'What would you offer?'

'For the exclusive contract of Harry Selfridge we will give you one hundred thousand pounds cash – no signatures for the cash. If you will give your lawyer instructions to make out a contract making me, Frank Farrell, the exclusive manager of Harry Selfridge I will give you in exchange one hundred thousand pounds – in cash. You could remain as his manager at a fixed salary.'

Solly kept on blinking wondering whether he had said the right thing, he might be making a mistake, he decided to see how far he could go with Farrell, but Farrell took over.

'Look Mr Segal – you have had your boy only a few months, one hundred grand is a lot of profit for a pop singer, they have ways of fizzling out after a year or so, either the kids get tired of them or somebody new comes along. I'm not here to waste time, I have to be in the States tomorrow night, I will be gone for a week – I have till the morning at noon, if you can come up with the contract I can come up with the cash. I am not doing any more bargaining – if you want to sell me your boy's contract I will buy it. If not, we have not wasted too much of each other's time. Let me know by twelve tomorrow.' He ushered Solly towards the door, shook hands with him and closed the door.

Farrell had seen that hooked look many times before on prisoners' faces, how they warped when you put the take it or leave it bite on them, he hadn't been a tobacco baron for nothing.

He felt confident that Solomon Segal would be in touch again before the day was out. Farrell flopped on the settee and began to work out his next move.

I made my way towards Solly's office in Bond Street, it was three-thirty, I hadn't been up long. When I walked in he jumped as if I had goosed him.

'What's up Solly?'

'Nothing,' he said and began biting his nails.

'I've never seen you bite your nails before.'

He shoved his hands quickly into his jacket pocket. 'Harry,' he said after clearing his throat several times, 'how would you like to make a quick ten grand – for nothing?'

'Ten grand! For nothing? What have you got in mind – robbing a bank?'

'No, you see Harry – in this business sometimes a promoter comes along and wants your exclusive services and he pays for that service, like a football club buys a player ...'

'Oh, I see ...' I said 'I see' but I didn't really see.

He went on. 'An organisation wants to buy your services for ten thousand pounds – that's cash in your pocket – no tax – nothing – all bunce!'

'What happens to *you*?' I asked.

'I stay and manage you, do all the bookings etcetera.'

'Where does your money come from?'

'They give me a couple of grand for myself.'

'Oh,' I said.

'Oh what?' said Solly.

'Well, you know, I'll do whatever you say – as long as I don't get into trouble.'

'What trouble?' said Solly quickly.

'I don't know – I don't care who I'm with as long as I earn a few quid, and I could do a few things with ten grand in my pocket.'

Solly said, 'Okay, I'll have a word with the people, I'll need your signature on a new sole agency agreement.'

He produced a contract that said I would be handled by a Frank Farrell who would take twenty-five per cent of my earnings in return for ten pounds.

'Why only ten pounds?' I asked.

'The rest is in cash Harry – if you put that in the contract you'll have to pay tax on it, that means they'll take the lot!'

'Oh,' I said again and put my signature at the bottom of the contract, above Solly's. I then borrowed two hundred pounds from him. For some reason Solly was perspiring freely. 'You all right Solly?' I asked.

' 'Course I'm all right.'

'You look hot – have you got a cold?'

'Er – I might have – I feel a little bit funny.'

'I'd better blow then, I don't want to catch it!' He laughed, but I'm sure he didn't hear what I said, he probably had some deal on his mind. I left and walked out into the fumes of the Bond Street traffic, all set to spend the two hundred quid.

13

Farrell answered the 'phone at four-twenty, he let it ring a few times before he picked up the receiver. 'Frank Farrell speaking.'

'Solomon Segal – Solly.'

'What is it Solly?'

'You said this morning that if I sold you our contract you'd keep me as manager – is that still on?'

'Certainly, I know nothing about management. I'd need you to handle Harry – anyway he knows you – he trusts you – sure Solly. What if we agree on a year's contract at say – er – five thousand a year plus expenses?'

'Five thousand a year?'

'Yeah, that way if you don't like me or I don't like you we aren't obligated to each other for life – it's a fair offer.'

'Um-um—' Solly tried to stall.

'What do you mean um-um? Don't lose sight of the fact that you will have one hundred thousand pounds cash up front – you either have an easy life right from the beginning or you work your arse off for the Exchequer for the next ten years and probably never see that much. You could invest at eleven per cent – that would bring you eleven grand a year and you'd still retain your capital. What do you mean um-um?'

'When can we do the deal?' said Solly after a short silence.

'I have a business meeting tonight and tomorrow I will have to get an associate to pick up the money from the bank. I have to check out at midday, could we make it eleven-thirty?'

'I'll be there at eleven-thirty Frank.'

'Okay Solly – I'll look forward to seeing you – don't forget to bring the contract Solly.'

'All right Frank – don't forget the money.'

They both laughed and hung up.

Farrell thought deeply for several minutes, then made two 'phone calls, one was to the hall porter asking for the loan of some scissors, the second was to one, Nipper Davis who had done five stretches for grievous bodily harm. Nipper would mug or rough anybody up for the price of two hundred quid. Farrell asked him to meet him at eight o'clock that evening outside the Playboy Club, he had a job for him.

'Fanks Frank,' said Nipper. 'I could do with it – the game's very quiet at the moment.'

The scissors arrived and Farrell spread out his entire wealth, five thousand pounds in twenties, less what he had paid for the suite that morning.

He began to cut the morning newspapers into the shape of the twenty pound notes, in another half an hour he had stacks of newspaper cuttings. He placed several genuine notes on top of each package and put them into an executive type briefcase he had purchased earlier in the day.

The effect was staggering, by raising the lid quickly it looked as if the briefcase contained hundreds and hundreds of twenty pound notes. He locked the case with the key and put it in his pocket.

He then ordered dinner. After he had eaten he wandered out on to Park Lane towards the Playboy Club, in the distance he could see the big form of Nipper Davis shuffling along the pavement.

Next day at eleven-thirty sharp Solly arrived at the suite again.

'Hi Solly!' shouted Farrell from the bathroom. 'Help yourself to some champagne – there's some in the ice bucket – be with you in a minute.'

Solly sat in the same armchair he had sat in the day before. While he waited he went over what he had been thinking ever since Farrell made his offer.

He would give Harry his ten thousand, he would give another ten grand to his old mother who lived over at Golders Green. For the past ten years he hardly missed visiting her on a Friday night to eat her chicken soup. One day, he'd promised her, he would make her really comfortable, he'd keep her in the manner a Jewish lady should be kept. A mink, a chauffeur, a daily help, ten grand wouldn't do it all but it would be a start. He suddenly wondered whether he was being a bit too kind to Harry, he had felt guilty not remunerating him fully after negotiating such a good deal. He shrugged, after all a short while ago he was a milkman, ten thousand in cash should make any milkman happy – why was he worrying about Harry? Harry was going to make plenty. He shrugged again and gulped his champagne then refilled his glass. He looked at the label on the bottle, one thing he felt sure of, this was his drink in the future.

'Sorry Solly,' said Farrell as he entered the room drying his hands. 'Been on the 'phone all morning.'

He threw the towel on the settee and walked towards a closet, he returned with the briefcase.

He fumbled for the key and undid the case, before he raised the lid he turned to Solly and said confidentially, 'There's a lot of money in here, it has been counted to the penny – one hundred thousand ...' Farrell was lifting the lid but kept talking, he was using one of the oldest confidence tricks known, keep the mug talking and his eyes looking into yours, he had already selected the part of the room where there was the least light. ' ... Solly – what I would like you to do is take this back to your office – count it ...' He lifted the lid of the case to let Solly have a good look, when he thought he had seen enough of the stacks of money, he gripped his arm, looked into his eyes again, snapped the case shut and continued, '... when you have counted it – put it into a safe deposit – don't put it into a bank otherwise you might have the revenue boys asking a lot of questions.' As Farrell said all this he was locking the case again. He held the key in front of Solly's eyes then said, 'Here you are, the key, the money, – it's all yours – all I need now is the contract.'

Solly took the key and the case, he was slightly bewildered at the speed with which things were happening. 'I thought we ought to have a talk.'

'I'd love to but I have to be on a plane in an hour, we'll talk when we get back. Did you bring the contract?'

Solly fished it out from an inner pocket. 'Here it is – it's all in order, signed by me and Harry, it's just an ordinary sole agreement – a standard contract.'

'Okay Solly – you will be careful with that loot won't you.'

'Don't worry – I'll guard it with my life.'

'I'll see you in a week – I'm coming down myself to check out.' Farrell took Solly by the arm and steered him towards the elevator.

They rode in the lift to the ground floor. Farrell walked with Solly to the entrance and stood there while the doorman called him a taxi.

' 'Bye Solly.'

' 'Bye Frank – you'll be in touch in a week, is that right?'

'That's right! See y'soon.'

120

The cab pulled away. Farrell watched as it disappeared and noticed the red Cortina begin to tail it. Sitting in the passenger seat he could make out the unmistakable bulk of Nipper Davis.

Farrell settled his bill for the incidentals he'd had up in the suite, and then made his way towards a pub at the bottom end of Edgware Road.

An hour later as he stood at the bar drinking a gin and tonic, in walked Nipper Davis with the briefcase he had handed to Solly just over sixty minutes before.

Nipper put it beside Farrell's feet. Farrell drank his drink, had a look round the almost empty bar, slipped an envelope with two hundred quid to Nipper, picked up the briefcase, and left. Neither of them spoke. Farrell hailed a cab and gave the driver an address in Highbury.

In the cab, he produced another key, opened the case, took out all the notes and put them in his pocket. He stopped the cab at the bottom of the road, paid the driver and watched it drive off.

After wiping the case all over for any fingerprints, he dropped the cut newspapers into a street dustbin. He made his way to the block of flats he was living in. Before going up to the fourth floor he went to the basement, he could feel from the heat that the incinerator was going full blast. He opened the grate door and pushed the briefcase into the flames. He wiped his hands and took the lift up to his apartment. It seemed hard to believe he had been away only a little over twenty-four hours.

He walked into the poky living-room and wished he was back at the suite in the Hilton.

With my dark glasses on I swung up Bond Street, towards Marble Arch, I felt good, in the mood for anything. A few people turned wondering where they'd seen me before. I made towards the flat and without any preamble I dialled

Dutton's Dairies. Eileen herself answered. 'Hello, Miss Dutton.' She knew it was me right away.

'Hello, Harry Selfridge – how's our star?'

'I'm great,' I kidded.

'What do we owe this great pleasure to?' she asked. I could almost hear the smile on her face.

'I wondered whether I could take you out for a meal.'

'Oh that's nice – when?'

'Tonight – when you finish.'

'Thank you Harry – what time?'

We made a date for eight and I told her I'd pick her up at Dutton's. I had a shower, shave, got ponced up and read some trade papers for an hour. At seven-thirty I took a cab over to Dutton's Dairies and there she stood – once again, the old apple tart started going ten to the dozen. I asked the cab to hang on and we made our way back to the West End.

'You look good Harry,' she said, as she gazed at me, I thought, rather fondly.

'You look good too Miss Dutton.'

She laughed and said, 'This Miss Dutton bit has got to go otherwise I'm going to call you Mr Selfridge – it's Eileen.'

'Okay Eileen.'

'Okay Harry. Where are we going?'

'Well Solly – you know Solly my manager? He took me to a club the other night and they made me a member, it's called the Twenty-One Club and it's in Mayfair.'

'Ooh. It sounds nice.'

I told the driver to go to the Twenty-One. They found us a table for two, it was early and the restaurant was half full. I had learned to let the maitre d. suggest the menu and this fellow who took our order had us both drooling.

We settled for Chateaubriand steaks with a bottle of

Nuits St George. For the first course we had jumbo-sized prawns which we dipped in mayonnaise, I made her laugh as I pretended to drink out of the fingerbowls.

We finished on Remy Martin brandies, looking up into each other's eyes. The boss of the place, Mr Meadows, sent us a bottle of Moet Chandon. We talked, I found out that the dairy could only exist a couple of months more. She didn't tell me this in a sad way, the way we both felt nothing could have spoiled that evening. We only noticed how late it was when the waiters began to stack the chairs on the tables.

I paid the bill which was a fortune, but the way I felt I wouldn't have cared if it had cost two fortunes. I tipped the waiters liberally and they bowed us out to the door where the doorman was waiting with a taxi. 'Where to?' he asked. Before she could reply I said, 'My place or yours?'

I expected to get a laugh but she quite seriously said, 'Yours.'

I gave the driver my address. We got in the cab and went into a clinch, her lips were soft and yielding. She ran her hands up the back of my neck and we stayed like that until the driver said, 'You two gonna be at it all night?' I bunged him a couple of quid and managed to get a half smile from him.

As we lay in bed exhausted from our love-making, I knew that this was what I had been looking for, oh it had been all right with other girls, but this was something else. Her gentleness, then her passion, then her surrender, all of it was beautiful. She felt the same way too, we were both very much in love.

It was the knock at the door that brought me out of my dream world, apart from the Daily, nobody had ever knocked at that door, not even the postman.

I saw panic in her eyes at the thought of being caught in bed naked, she grabbed the sheet and pulled it up to her neck. We lay there and the knock came again, more urgently. I slipped my slacks on and went to the door.

Outside stood a fellow with oily hair, a cigarette dangling from his lips, in a suit that went out with Marty Wilde. He grinned and showed several teeth missing, 'Hello Harry.'

'Hello,' I said, 'do I know you?'

'Harry,' he pleaded, his palms stretched towards me.

The light wasn't that good and I had come from the dimly-lit bedroom.

I said, 'Look, I don't want to play guessing games at this time of the night, who are you?'

'Harry,' he said, 'I'm Daddy.'

'Who?'

'Your daddy.'

Solly had no idea what hit him as he walked into his office in Bond Street. He went over the event as he nursed the back of his neck. He'd got in the taxi in Park Lane holding the briefcase, the taxi had stopped outside his office. He remembered paying the taxi with a pound note and waiting while the cabbie fiddled to give him change, vaguely he remembered a red car stopping behind the taxi and a big man getting out from the offside.

He could recollect grasping the case tight, walking into the darkened doorway and ascending the stairs, that's all he *could* remember. He felt the chop across his neck and everything going black. Five minutes later when he came to, the briefcase was gone. Not a soul had entered or left the building who might have seen him lying there.

Now he was in his office, his secretary had put a cold flannel on his neck, she had 'phoned the police and they were waiting for them to arrive.

Solly sat there with his head in his hands wondering how he could have made and lost one hundred thousand pounds in a day. Another frightening thing occurred to him, how could he tell the police he had lost all that money? When the sergeant took particulars, he told them that the case had just a few personal belongings and some papers, he thought it wiser not to mention the money at that particular moment.

The ironical part was, as he sat here, the 'phone was ringing with enquiries about Harry Selfridge. As he began to negotiate salaries of twelve thousand pounds for a week's engagement, he suddenly realised that he didn't represent him any more, he had signed him away on the piece of paper he had given to Frank Farrell; all he was doing was the office boy's work, the real percentages would go to the new manager, Farrell. He put his head on the desk and sobbed uncontrollably.

'Your father! I'm your father Harry – don't you remember?'

I gazed at him and he was chirping like a cricket.

'You haven't forgotten all those days over at Battersea Park have you Harry? All those rides on the big dipper – the tree walk – all those mirrors that make you look fat and thin? Christ, we never used to miss a day in the summer.'

It began to come slowly back to me, he would give me a few bob to go on all the roundabouts and fun fairs then he'd skip off and search for all the stray crumpet that was around. Most days I had to find my own way back home. I could have only been six or seven.

'And now my Harry boy's a star.' He shoved out a scrawny hand that had a deceptively strong grip.

'Harry – I've been up here half a dozen times but you've always been out. I thought I'd come here tonight on the offchance. I want a job Harry, could you use me? I'll do anything – roadie – driver – stage manager – anything!'

'Come and see me tomorrow,' I said, 'I'm a bit tired at present!'

He began to protest but I shut the door.

I wandered back into the bedroom, Eileen had got into her dress and was sitting on the side of the bed.

'Anything wrong Harry?'

'I've just met my father.'

'I didn't know you had a father.'

'Neither did I.'

'I think I ought to go Harry – it's very late.'

I didn't argue, although I would have loved to have gone back to bed cradled in her arms like we'd been before my visitor came.

I took her down to the street and flagged a taxi. She begged me not to come with her as it was late. I kissed her goodnight and she promised to ring me. I waved goodbye and should have been thinking of her as she disappeared down the Edgware Road, but a voice from a doorway called, 'Don't forget tomorrow Harry!' I turned to see my father lighting up a new cigarette from another stub. 'Cheerio son!' he called as he too disappeared down the Edgware Road.

As I dropped off to sleep my mind was a tangled mess of thoughts, I could see my father's face, a Brylcreem advert, that awful film about smoking and lung cancer and in the background I could hear the Eddie Calvert trumpet playing 'O mein papa'.

'I was mugged,' said Solly to Frankie Farrell.

'Mugged – you're kidding – people don't get mugged in broad daylight in Bond Street.'

'I tell you it's true Frank – they took the case and

the money and left me lying on the stairs. It's a wonder I'm alive – what can we do?' He held the 'phone showing white knuckles.

'What d'ye mean what can *we* do? I gave you a hundred thousand in notes – did you call the police?'

'Yes I called them but I only told them I'd lost the briefcase.'

'Thank God for that – you'd have had them asking both of us a lot of awkward questions.' Frank hid his sigh of relief.

'I've fixed Harry up with work for the next three months – I have booked him for club dates, Television and concerts, he has got the best part of two hundred thousand if you include his record royalties.'

'OK,' said Farrell. 'Send me copies of the contracts and I will vet them – make sure all cheques are made out to Frank Farrell Entertainments.'

'Frank!' said Solly. 'What about all that money that went?'

'Look Solly I paid you fair and square. If you gamble, or lose it or give it away that's your business, we owe each other nothing – send me those contracts, to my office.'

Solly remained speechless, then after a long silence he said, 'All right Frank – where shall I send them?'

'Send them to the Hilton Hotel.'

'Okay Frank,' Solly said dismally.

'Oh and Solly – from now on I think it ought to be Mister Farrell – okay?'

'Okay – Mister Farrell.'

Solly hung up and once more the tears came, this time he banged his head on the desk to shut out the awful thoughts.

14

For the next three months I was working in a way I had never dreamed would be possible. It was hard graft but enjoyable – well it was enjoyable at first but I began to get a little bored towards the end. Disc jockeys asked me the same questions.

'How does it feel having the Number One record?'

'Oh, it feels great.'

'Are you going to make another one soon?'

'Yes we're doing one soon!'

'What is it called?'

'I don't know you'll have to ask my manager Frankie Farrell.'

'How much do you make now Harry?'

'You'll have to ask my manager that too, he's in charge of all the finance.'

'I believe you have your father working for you now.'

'Yes, he helps me on these gigs.'

'Do you have any girlfriends?'

'Oh yes – lots.'

'Anyone you are likely to lead up the aisle?'

'No, not at present.'

'So all your fans have a chance yet, eh Harry?'

I usually laughed when they said this, it was only way to be non-committal. Everybody thought I was getting my oats every night of the week, I wasn't. The two people doing the best in the crumpet stakes was the old man, who was now working as a roadie for me, he chatted these little groupies up and then took them back to his caravan.

The other was Frankie Farrell, who usually stood at

the back of the theatre or club puffing on a Havana corona, then when he saw a likely one in the audience who looked like she was on her own, he'd chat her up and whip her back to his hotel with the promise that they'd meet me after the show.

Since the night Eileen and me had been together I just didn't have the patience for any other girl, I was dying for this tour to end so I could see her again.

I was being paid two thousand pounds a week by Frankie Farrell. He paid this into a bank account at a bank near my flat in London.

Unknown to Eileen I had paid ten thousand pounds into her bank account, with a promise from her bank manager not to say where it had come from. At least she could keep the dairy going, I 'phoned her periodically and we had long chats on the 'phone.

I had my father on salary that was paid by the Frank Farrell office. He was a great help and in some strange way I found myself liking him more and more.

Solly never came out on the road, he was very morose lately, he just made the bookings and let me know where they were.

Catgut took the orchestra rehearsals and all I had to do was turn up and perform. The audience mostly consisted of girls and women, who cheered and clapped everything I did.

My father was stuffing a different bird every night, Frank Farrell was having parties back at his hotel which I avoided, Catgut got as high as a kite on the weed he was puffing after every performance, and the result was that after I had been driven back to the hotel I was usually alone. I became an avid reader. At first I read mysteries and thrillers but then I became hooked on some of the greats like Galsworthy, Michener and Thurber; then I turned to autobiographies. I learned quite a lot

129

from writers like Churchill, Priestley and Dickens, in fact, anything that was readable I read. I found I could finish a book in two or three days.

What began to worry me was the newspapers had suddenly stopped praising any effort I was making to get my act more acceptable, few of them wrote about our concerts or club engagements, it seemed they were always more eager to find out who I was sleeping with. They wrote up Frank Farrell's parties as though I was the life and soul of them, in fact I was back in my hotel room reading a book. When I remarked on it to Farrell he put his arm round my shoulder and told me the time to worry was when the papers ignored me.

One article that got me particularly worried was the one that appeared on a Sunday and told the world that my manager was an ex-jailbird who had done several terms in jail for armed robbery.

They made a feast of telling how he had been in Borstal as a sixteen-year-old, then jail sentence followed jail sentence. I was amazed to read that of the past ten years, eight of them had been spent as a guest of Her Majesty's Prisons.

I began wondering how a man like this had become my manager. I remembered Solly telling me that I was going to get ten thousand in cash when I signed the new contract in his office that day. He had never given it to me but I wasn't unduly worried, I thought things like that took time, anyway I was making a lot of money, over two thousand pounds a week. I had read that I had been paid fifteen thousand for one week at a certain club, but was assured by Farrell that this was only newspaper talk to convince the readers I was a hot property.

He told me he had been working on my behalf with our accountants about setting up an offshore company. I didn't quite understand, but it seemed that a company was to be formed in the Cayman Islands which would contract my services for a small sum. Then all the big fees that I earned would be channelled into it. This way I would not be eligible for tax in Great Britain and would make a big saving.

Another thing that worried me was when Farrell explained that I might have to give up being a resident in England for at least a year to justify this tax fiddle. When I mentioned this word, he was quick to point out it was not a fiddle, it is every citizen's duty to pay tax, but if he or she can 'avoid' tax, it is also a duty.

With his record I was not too sure, but he was not a man I cared to tangle with, his physique was enough to convince me he could have eaten me for breakfast. Almost every idea he dreamed up, I went along with, it always seemed so plausible.

I began to become inquisitive only when Eileen stopped taking my 'phone calls, at first I left messages for her to call me back, she didn't, but when I began to get person to person calls rejected I knew that she didn't want to talk to me.

I could only assume it was because of the newspapers' articles that had suddenly referred to my antics and of Farrell, Catgut and my father as The Sewer Sect.

We certainly had a bad name.

It amazed me that it didn't keep the audiences away; the worse the articles became, the longer the queues got. When I walked on the stage there were cries of ecstasy from the women, the fellows didn't do too badly either.

It was when I looked in the mirror in the bathroom for a long time one morning and studied my face, I suddenly realised what was missing – the humour had gone.

Frank Farrell couldn't believe how easily the money was coming in. In the past three months he had netted over one hundred thousand pounds for himself, Solly had received an offer from America for Harry to do a tour of thirty cities that would net him one million dollars.

He had made several enquiries to various accountants and had finished up with a team of experts who had guaranteed to save him most, if not all of that. All he had to do was keep Harry happy, keep him healthy and here was a meal ticket for the next few years at least.

During the first few weeks he had stood in the background and let Solly do the engagements, but gradually he had eased him out so that all deals for Harry had to be made personally through him.

It was the day after the article appeared about him being an ex-jailbird that the first spot of bother began. Solly had obviously read the article and had been doing a lot of thinking, he could tell by the way the meeting went that Monday in his suite.

'Mr Farrell, I have brought the standard contracts you wanted.'

'Thank you Mr Segal.' There was no first name basis with them any more.

'Did you see the article yesterday?' asked Solly.

'Yes I saw it – so what?'

'Are you going to sue?'

'How can I sue – it's the truth.'

'It won't help Harry too much, you know he has a big teenage following – somebody has been referring to his company as The Sewer Sect, it can't help his image too much – parents will be reluctant to let their kids go to his concerts.'

'Parents weren't too mad about Mick Jagger and Joe Cocker at first – but it didn't hurt *them*,' said Farrell.

'But Harry was a nice guy six or eight weeks ago – suddenly he's got the tag of a sewer rat – that's got to be bad.'

'Take it from me Segal – the public love a villain – they love him twice as much if he's a successful villain.'

'Well I er ...'

Farrell cut in, 'Look Segal, Sinatra's clan was called the Rat Pack – Sammy Davis, Dean Martin, Sinatra himself – loved booze, broads and trouble – every one of them is big box office today – bigger than they would have been if they'd been thumping bibles. Since Harry got what you call bad publicity the box office has doubled – we've had enquiries from Australia, France, America, Germany – they all want to book him – because he's alive – he's vibrant – if they want a sermon they'd have booked Billy Graham.'

'But Harry's a nice kid – there's plenty of money coming in, we don't need to push him ...'

'Look Mr Segal!' Farrell brought his hand down on the table, '... don't tell me how to run my boy – if you are against what I do, leave the organisation and I will do the bookings myself – you have had your money ...'

'I haven't had *any* money!' It was Solly's turn to shout. 'I paid you one hundred thousand pounds!'

'You may have paid it to me – but you or somebody you know had it back off me fifteen minutes later.'

'That's a terrible accusation you've made Mr Segal.' Farrell was glaring.

'Shit Farrell – only you and I knew what was in that briefcase when I left the hotel.'

'I happen to have witnesses at that very hotel – like the porter, the doorman, the girl at the news-stand and a taxi driver that could swear I didn't leave that hotel until a good half hour after you.' Farrell had tipped all four liberally before he left asking each one the time, telling them he had to catch a plane in one hour – he had also asked the doorman to put his watch right for him on the pretence that he couldn't read the hands with-

133

out his glasses. Each of them would have an indelible memory of the times, you don't forget anybody that tips like that in a hurry, especially for just telling the time. Farrell knew he would be on safe ground should Solly Segal ever get suspicious.

'Well if it wasn't you, you had an accomplice and I intend to get the C.I.D. in and let them sort it out. I have been chiselled out of my cut, out of my agency and out of my artiste, all I have to show is a lousy salary of £100 a week – by rights all you have belongs to me – I am not a complete mug and in the next few days you'd better have a good story ready for the police – because Mr Farrell they will be asking you questions.'

'Like what?' asked Farrell quietly.

'Like where *you* got one hundred thousand in readies – where you went to in America when you were supposed to have left here and quite a few other things . . .'

Solly threw down the papers he was holding, was about to say some more, thought better of it and made for the door, slamming it as he left. Farrell watched him go and began to feel uneasy, the last thing he wanted was the C.I.D. snooping round. Not now, not with, literally, the key of the Bank of England in his hands.

He thought for a long time then slowly dialled the number of Nipper Davis.

I didn't know what to expect, the Cayman Islands sounded rather romantic. We had left London Airport that morning and changed planes at Miami.

There was a main street that had names of banks from all over the world, The Chase Manhattan, Bank of Nova Scotia, Bank of Montreal, Barclays etcetera.

We were ushered into a tiny air-conditioned office which made me wish I had my jacket, which I'd left back at the hotel.

I had been bitten badly on the neck by mosquitos and they were itching like crazy.

The lawyer's name was Sadler, he asked for my signature on several documents, Farrell was sitting beside me and as I began to read what I was signing he said, 'It's okay Harry – they've all been vetted – just put your moniker across the seals.'

'I'd rather read them first Frank.'

'Okay but there's really no need – that right Mr Sadler?'

'Well, we did exactly as you asked Mr Farrell.'

'Will you explain it to Harry so he knows exactly what we are doing.'

I put the documents on my knee and listened to Mr Sadler explain in a lot more detail that I was forming a company that would have directors in the Cayman Islands who were residents. All monies that I earned would go to a trust, of which we would become beneficiaries, half would go to Farrell and half to me.

'It doesn't seem right for a half to go to Mr Farrell does it Mr Sadler? After all I am the one who's earning it.'

I felt Farrell stiffen in the chair beside me, he turned to Sadler and said, 'Will you please excuse us for a few minutes, Mr Sadler.'

Sadler left.

As the door closed Farrell turned to me and said, 'What's the big fucking idea!'

'I think fifty per cent of my earnings is a lot to pay.'

'At fifty per cent you will make fifty thousand pounds on a hundred grand.'

'If I paid you ten per cent like other acts do, I'd make ninety thousand.'

'Look son, there's a lot of things you don't know about this racket – first, I paid Solly Segal a lot of blood for your contract – one hundred thousand pounds I gave him.

One hundred thousand . . . you understand that?' He said it as if he was doing an impression of Rod Steiger. 'Now that's a lot of loot – I paid that out as an investment – I want to get some interest on my outlay.'

'I should think you've had that back by now Frank – on my engagements in England alone.'

'Look fucking glamour boy!' He had turned really sour now like he was sucking a lemon. 'Look, what I've made is no fucking concern of yours – you have a contract to honour which will hold water in any court on earth, it states that you will pay me fifty fucking per cent of all earnings – it's a watertight contract!'

'That's in England Frank, this is a different contract, it's in the Cayman Islands.'

'That's got fuck all to do with it!' He had gone blood-red even in that air-conditioned room.

'And there's no need to keep swearing,' I said.

'I'll swear when I fucking well like,' he shouted.

'All right Frank,' I said quietly. 'We'll forget the contract and go back to England . . .'

'Listen you tuppenny ha'penny pop singer – we go back to England – we'll be taxed on everything we make – we might as well be digging ditches – I've been setting this up for weeks – months – we can keep the lot after we have paid the withholding tax in any country we work – we'll make a million dollars—'

'So at ten per cent – you make a hundred thousand – that's not a bad return on your money – on your original investment.'

His eyes shot up at my knowledge of all this.

'How did you know about all this?'

I could have told him I had spent several nights talking to my father, he had an idea of the salary the clubs were paying me and the money that Farrell was taking for his cut. He also knew a few of the villains that Farrell associated with and had warned me not to get on the wrong side of him, but on this day I felt rebellious.

'Oh I keep my ears open,' I said.

He looked at me with a mixture of admiration and hate – he looked for a long time. Then without a word he walked to the door and called Mr Sadler back.

'There's been a mistake Mr Sadler – ninety per cent of the trust will go to Mr Selfridge and ten per cent to myself.'

We walked out into the ninety-seven degrees of heat back to the hotel. On the way he announced that I would have to become a non-resident of Britain for a year and a day.

We flew back to London, packed a few belongings and left again for the first tour of the United States. As I mounted the steps of the jumbo I found it hard to believe that I wouldn't be seeing my country for another year – no more journeys up and down the motorways, no BBC radio – no rain or fog – at least not with that English taste – no more – I looked round at the observation platform where a few fans who had got wind of my departure were waving frantically. I gave them a wave and a big smile – then, I don't know if my eyes were playing tricks but right at the end of the railing I saw a girl just standing watching – it was Eileen Dutton – I think it was, I was asked to get a move on by some people behind, when I looked back she had gone.

15

Solly's secretary had taken a message for him to call his mother, he had tried for the past two hours but there was no answer. He decided to do a few more things in the office, tried once more to get her then decided he'd drive over to Golders Green and see her, perhaps the 'phone was out of order.

He had not yet been to the police. He knew he could get an investigation going, Farrell was a hard nut with a load of form behind him, the police would want to know where Farrell got all the money to give Solly.

Solly was thinking as he steered the car up Finchley Road that perhaps if he scared Farrell, things might be different. He must show him he was not to be meddled with, even if Farrell was a criminal he was in England, this wasn't America – those Mafia-type tactics would not do in a country like ours.

He was surprised to see no lights on as he stopped the car outside the door. He knocked, got no reply so sorted out the key from the large bunch he carried to unlock the street door.

He switched the light on in the hall and called up the stairs, 'Mama!' The house was still. 'Mama you there?'

He walked into the small living-room, switched on the light and gasped: his mother's immaculate room was a complete shambles, pictures were smashed, cushions had been ripped open, the contents had been thrown all round the room, pots of jam had been thrown at the walls, almost everything edible from the refrigerator had been thrown at the ceiling or walked into her green and gold carpet. Milk had been poured over her tiny sewing machine, a jar of honey lay smashed with its contents splattered over the velvet drapes in the bay window.

As he stood there taking in the destruction, he heard a whimper. He walked towards the settee that stood in the bay window, looked behind it, and there bound hand and foot with a large piece of sticking plaster across her mouth was his mother, looking up at him with frightened eyes.

He pulled the tape from her mouth, he was relieved to see she was unhurt. He undid the ropes around her.

'Mama – you all right?' She just clung to him. 'Oh Solomon,' she whispered. 'Oh Solomon – he was dreadful.'

'Who Mama?'

'This big man – gruff voice – asked if you were in – said it was about Harry Selfridge – I let him in – he put his hand over my mouth – he was like a gorilla—'

'What else Mama?'

'He tied me up – then started doing all this to the room – he was like a madman – kept laughing to himself all the time.'

She broke away from Solly and said, 'Why would anyone do this to me? I've never hurt a soul.'

The 'phone in the hall rang startling both of them. 'I'll get it Mama.' Solly picked up the 'phone and said, 'Yes, who is it?' A cockney voice in a mocking tone said, 'Hello-o-o, is that Solly Segal?'

'Who's that?' asked Solly.

'Never mind who this is sonny boy – I just want you to know that if you've got any ideas about going to the police about anything at all you'd better forget it – else the next time you see your mother she won't be tied up behind a settee – she'll be dead – ta-ta Solly.'

139

There was a click and the 'phone went dead. Solly walked back into the room and told his mother to pack a few things, he would put her up in an hotel while the place was being cleaned up.

'Aren't you going to 'phone the police Solomon?'

'I'll do it all – the first thing to do is get you out of here.'

He waited for her to pack, then drove her to a small hotel in Maida Vale where she was comfortable. Then he got in his car and made for the Hilton, he wished he had a gun, he'd shoot Farrell down as he opened his door without any questions.

He parked the car and marched into the hotel, he made his way to the penthouse suite.

He banged on the door, there was no reply, a maid appeared in the corridor.

'You looking for Mr Farrell?'

'Yes I am.'

'He's gone to America – he checked out this morning.'

'You sure?'

She nodded. Solly, deflated, walked out of the hotel and into his car.

As he drove home he thought how near he had been to murder. He consoled himself with the adage – 'everything comes to him who waits'.

The rest of them called him my old man, but I could never call him that or dad or pop or father, I called him what the rest of them did – Reg.

Since he had been working for me, or our organisation, he had made himself indispensable, he was the best little worker I knew.

As soon as the concert was over, he would wrap up the consoles, coil up all the leads and have the instruments and music stands into the back of the van inside the hour.

In the few months he had been with us he had altered his appearance radically, the greasy hair was gone, so was that 1950 gear he wore. His hair was dry, long, plentiful and washed regularly.

He had had his teeth fixed, the gaps had been filled, he now had a wide good-natured smile. I think he must have heard about my dislike for smoking because he never smoked a cigarette near me.

Somehow I felt he wanted to get closer to me, at most of the gigs we did I usually said, 'Hi Reg – you all right?' He would reply, 'Fine thanks Harry,' then get on with what he was doing.

On the tour of America our entourage was made up of Farrell, Catgut Lowery, a drummer who had also joined us named Dave Summers, myself and Reg. We were to use an American pianist and also a bass guitarist when we got to New York.

Farrell sat down in the front row in the first class section of the jumbo, I sat behind him. They usually left me alone on long flights because they knew I liked to read, so Catgut and Reg sat about four rows back, the plane was only a third full so there were quite a few empty seats.

I looked up to see Reg standing there. 'Can I sit down for a minute Harry?' I moved some magazines and papers. Here Reg – make yourself at home.'

'Good flight ain't it,' he said as he sat down.

'You can hardly feel these jets,' I said, making small talk.

'You all right Harry?'

'All right? What d'ye mean?'

'You look a little bit down nowadays – like you're not

enjoying it all – anything worrying you?' He studied me waiting for my reply.

'I'm all right – I'm a bit of a loner – that's all.'

'You always were,' he said, 'you were never one for organised games, you used to go to pictures by yourself, play football by yourself, you were never one for the gang.'

'I suppose you should know.'

'I don't know if she ever said anything to you Harry but when a couple break up it's usually because it's half a dozen of one and six of the other – they're both to blame. It was like that with me and your mum.'

'She never said a lot,' I smiled.

'We both were too young when we got spliced. She was the one that wanted to go out every night, apart from the expense I couldn't do it – I was working – I had to be ready for work next day – she could have a kip, sleep in till four if she liked. Then she started going out without me – when she knew you were on the way she went raving mad, but she had you as easy as shelling peas – do you know, a week – only a week after you were born she went to an all-night party down at the Bricklayers Arms, she didn't get home till six – and that was only to give you your first feed.'

We both laughed and he went on talking.

'I'm not saying she was to blame because I was twice as bad – I was having it off left, right and centre, but when the break came the one bloody thing that broke my heart was you.'

'How d'ye mean?'

'Well Harry, I don't care who it is, if a man has a son he sees little things in him that nobody else sees – he notices the way he walks, breathes, sniffs, notices his kindnesses, his wickedness – everything. You're a smashing kid Harry.'

142

I said, 'Aaaah shuttup!'

He didn't laugh, he said again. 'You are Harry – you've done some lovely things with your success – you've looked after me – I know you look after the old lady.'

'There's nothing else to do with it – except give it away,' I shrugged.

'Don't forget your old age Harry – nobody gives you anything when you need it ...' He got closer to me to make sure Farrell sitting in front of us couldn't hear. Don't be a mug with these fellows, they're cruel bastards, they don't put them away in prisons for years for their health – be careful Harry – I'm not crawling or looking for anything but if I can ever be of any help – anytime – anywhere – just whistle – don't forget son.'

'I won't Reg,' I said.

He got up and went back to his seat.

My arrival in New York surprised even us. We had seen what could happen in England, kids had gone berserk there but this was unbelievable, mounted police had horses up on their hind legs trying to get the crowds back, cameramen were fighting each other to get the best angles of me as I came off the plane.

The customs men turned us inside out.

'Why are they doing all this?' I said to Reg.

'Drugs – they're looking for drugs.' He let me see his eyes shift towards Catgut. We all waited while the customs man went through Catgut's cases as though he had a small tooth comb.

Eventually they let us through, the officer's parting words were, 'I hope you're gonna behave yourself while you're in our country Mr Selfridge.' He smiled, the smile of one of those who had read about and didn't care too much for, the Sewer Sect.

'I'll try,' I smiled back. I heard Catgut hiss, 'Fuck off pig!' I was glad I was the only one that heard.

We were pushed and shoved and clouted, some clot tried to interview us in the lounge for television, I couldn't get a word in. I tried to answer his questions, a copper pushed me in the small of the back, I went arse over head and tried to come up smiling even though it had stunned me.

When I watched the TV four hours later in the hotel suite I could understand why quite a lot of people disliked me. I looked so grim-faced as I tried to get through the crowd, then when I went down, some guy had got his zoom lens on my face to make me look like an idiot.

I looked like a zombie as I surfaced, a stupid grin on my face as a dozen hands put me back on my feet – I looked like somebody that was drugged up to the eyeballs. No wonder churches all over America were crying out for my deportation.

Farrell was loving it, he thought it was great publicity for the coming tour. Some of the audiences at the concerts would number twelve or fifteen thousand people, Farrell's eyes looked like cash registers. It was to be hectic but lucrative, even I, who was not all that keen on the monetary side, was impressed.

All day the hotel suite was full of reporters and gossip writers plus cameramen and hangers-on, drinking from the bar or eating the cooked food that was coming in regularly.

I answered the same questions over and over again, one woman reporter who looked like she took ugly pills asked, 'What are you drinking?'

'It's er – ginger ale.'

'Why ginger ale?'

'Because I like it.'

'Are you afraid of getting pissed?'

I had rarely heard a woman use that expression before, she waited for my reaction.

'Er no – not er really.'

'Does it cramp your style?'

'How do you mean?'

'Does it interfere with your fucking?' She was stony-faced as she said it. We looked at each other, neither of us spoke. I suddenly wanted to know what right this bitch had being so bloody rude. I poured myself a full glass of ginger ale.

'Will you answer my question?' The American nasal sound was really getting to me.

'What er question?'

The room had suddenly gone quiet and everybody was looking towards us.

'Does it interfere with your fucking?'

'Er does what do what?'

'Drinking ginger ale.'

'Try it and see.' I threw the whole glass into her face. I got up and walked into the bedroom.

In came a guy called Abe Sollas. 'You'd better apologise to her Harry.'

'Tell her to piss off.'

'She could do you a lot of harm.'

'That's too bad.'

'Look Harry, I'm the publicity for this tour, I have to keep these people sweet for my next client now be a good guy and tell her you're sorry. I beg of you.'

'She shouldn't have been so bloody rude.'

'She's looking for an angle, she is a great newspaper-woman – say you're sorry and she may soft pedal – otherwise she'll crucify you. Harry *please*, for me!'

I had cooled off. 'Okay what's her name?'

'Christine Grear – she's got a big following.'

I walked back into the room – she was still drying herself off with a napkin. I walked towards her, took the napkin and dried her myself. 'I'm sorry Christine, I apologise, it's been a long flight and I was tensed up.'

'You sure were,' she said.

'Will you forgive me?' I stood in mock shameface.

'How could I not forgive you.' She seemed to be enjoying the attention she was getting, then she kissed me on the cheek.

'You won't do it again will you, Harry?'

'Not unless I'm pissed!'

Everybody laughed.

America really was different – audiences were twice as enthusiastic as anything we'd had in Britain. The screams seemed higher, the security men who were employed to hold the kids back seemed like the Gestapo.

Even the spotlights seemed more powerful, the sound seemed to have more clarity and the gelatine that changed the colour of the lights seemed more vivid.

As I gazed into the void, picking out the reds, blues and greens of the arc lights I was always aware I was on foreign soil, I tried to sing well, trying to block out the screams and pitch my voice in tune with the musicians, it wasn't always easy but sometimes I managed it.

Strange how all those kids in that audience believed I was singing to them individually, when all the time the only vision I could conjure up was Eileen Dutton.

Commercially the tour was a big success, we were now in the middle of it – in Chicago.

Farrell had taken to smoking larger cigars and walked with me the way a manager leads a prize fighter. I got a little idea how nasty he could be one afternoon in the hotel.

Two middle-aged men were waiting to see him, they

talked from the sides of their mouths like old-time movie gangsters, they wore light grey suits and except for one having a good head of steel grey hair while the other was balding, could have been twins.

'What can I do for you gentlemen?' asked Farrell.

'Is Mr Selfridge having a successful tour?'

'I think you would say that – why?'

'Our card,' said the balding one.

He handed Farrell a card which I found out later told the recipient they were union bosses.

'We are responsible for the security, the stage staff, electricians, in fact everything that makes your tour the big success that it is.'

'Good,' said Farrell. 'You're doing a good job.'

'I feel sure, like you must do Mr Farrell, that considering the revenue you are garnishing here in Chicago you wouldn't be averse to show the boys your appreciation.'

'Like how?' asked Farrell.

'Like a donation to union funds.'

'How much?'

'A thousand dollars would be greatly appreciated.'

'What if I had come on this tour and we'd been losing money – would you have come along and given me or Mr Selfridge a thousand dollars?' asked Farrell with a smile.

They both looked at each other uncertainly, most promoters I learned paid over this blackmail without a peep, it would be a bit harder to get it from Farrell. I could sense he was looking for a bit of excitement.

'Supposing I don't feel like giving the boys a donation?'

'Well,' said Baldy, '... you may find one of the boys has accidentally failed to put the juice on – the spotlights could be outta commission and the security boys may be out for a smoke forgetting that the fans want to climb up on the stage.'

Farrell studied them both for a moment then said, 'Well, I'll tell you what I'll do gentlemen, you make sure that tonight's concert goes without a hitch and tomorrow before we leave Chicago there will be a donation waiting here – in fact if it goes very well – I may double the donation. Okay?' He held out his hand.

They got up smiling and shook hands all round.

'We'll be here before you check out tomorrow Mr Farrell. Have a good stay.'

'I will.' He walked to the door with his hands on their shoulders.

'That's quite a bite for a one night stand,' I said as Frank closed the door, 'you gonna pay it?'

'It's your money Harry – you don't want me to waste it do you?'

'They're union men – they could cause trouble.'

'Don't worry – tomorrow we'll be in another State.' He winked.

'But they'll be here in the morning.'

'Well they're gonna be unlucky aren't they?'

The party after the show that night was like an orgy, people sat around in the hotel room drinking, cuddling each other, men with men, women with women. I walked into the bathroom and found some stranger there, he had long flowing hair, a beard that had never been trimmed, he was humming quietly to himself – his left sleeve was rolled up, as I walked in he said, 'Hi Harry wanna roller coast with me?' He held up a hypodermic syringe. 'I got plenty baby.' 'No thanks,' I stammered, then stood there mesmerised as he shoved the needle into his arm. He washed the syringe, packed it back into a box, rolled his sleeve down then walked back into the room where the action was. I thought, 'Christ, all we want now is Elliot Ness to walk in and we'd all be put away for life.' I picked my way across the sprawling mass to my room down the corridor and tried to sleep.

I couldn't. I wondered what it was like in England. I could almost taste those early mornings in the autumn when the dawn broke slowly, the road sweepers pushing those large brooms to clear the gutters of fallen leaves to allow the rain, that would surely come, to run away down the drains. I could see the workers standing at bus stops shifting from one foot to another, sometimes blowing on their hands and threshing their arms. I could see the annoyance on their faces as they waited for an overdue bus then resignation when three buses came along at almost the same time.

I had only been away a little over two weeks – it seemed a lifetime. I had been to twelve cities in America but all I had seen of them was the view from a car window as I was hurtled from hotel to airport – from airport to hotel. How was I ever going to be able to stand a full year away? I was homesick already.

I thought about the word homesick – what was I homesick about? I didn't even have a home. I got up, went to the fridge and poured myself a glass of milk – that's the last thing I should have done – how can you go back to sleep with a glass of milk in one hand – the thoughts of the dairy at Battersea going through your mind and a great big yearning to be holding the boss in your arms? I went back to the party and got pissed.

I woke up with a king-sized hangover.

'Come on Harry,' shouted Farrell. 'We've got half an hour!'

I dressed as fast as I could.

We were about to go out of the door and walked straight into Bill and Ben – the union men.

'Looks like we're just in time – you haven't forgotten us have you Mr Farrell?'

'Of course not,' smiled Frank. 'Come in.' They came in, he closed the door, and at the same moment threw his raincoat into Baldy's face, the other one who hadn't bothered to take his hands out of his pockets suddenly got the ham fist of Farrell's right into his solar plexus, as he went down Farrell's knee sent him upright, while he was in that position Frank hit him twice, right on the point of the jaw, it was lights out for him, he lay there not making a move.

The grey-haired one had now untangled himself from the raincoat, and decided to leave when he saw his mate lying there. Farrell flew at him from behind and dragged his topcoat from his shoulders so that it was halfway down his back. He pushed him forward so his head cracked against the large oak door, he spun him round, all I could see was the fright in the American's eyes, Farrell hit him the same way as he hit the first man, two hooks left and right to the point of the chin, as he fell Farrell caught him in his arms, dragged him over to his friend and let him fall across him. The two of them lay there, it would be a long time before they surfaced.

'Come on Harry – we've got a plane to catch.' He was actually grinning to himself.

Not a day passed without Solly Segal going over the events of the day he was mugged. He was now more than sure that Farrell was behind it all.

He had been cheated of everything, but finding his mother bound and gagged had made him reluctant to get involved with the police, it was obvious that Farrell didn't play games. He thought about his mother who until the incident had been quite placid, the doctor had now put her on tranquillisers.

Solly had moved her to a small hotel at Brighton, as

far away as he could from the Golders Green episode, he hoped she would, in time, erase it from her memory. He had put the house up for sale.

His time was filled with some small acts he had taken on with Farrell's permission. There was a singer he could hardly raise a hundred pounds a week for, a juggler in the same bracket and a rock group he was managing to book one week in four – the whole lot of them hardly brought in twenty-five pounds a week in commission.

He thought of Harry Selfridge, Superstar! In one day he could have been earning more than he was getting from the crap he was handling in a year. Harry was the biggest single earner in the world at the moment, he tried to push it out of his mind but it was no use, he finished up the same way every day, head on his arms on top of the desk, sobbing.

We were booked at a place called the Cow Palace, an enormous arena in San Francisco. It was a week after we had left Chicago.

We had finished the concert and managed to return to the hotel in one piece. We had a few friends back but they left comparatively early. I said goodnight to Reg, Catgut and Farrell. I put the key in my door, reached for the light switch, suddenly bang! somebody hit me from behind. I fell to the floor, could dimly make out two figures, one picked me up and held me by the arms, the other one stood in front of me and hit me hard in the stomach, I thought I was going to spill my supper there and then.

'Listen you Limey bastard – tell Mr Farrell this is a little present from the boys in Chicago.' He brought his hand across my face and I could taste the blood streaming from my nose.

'Tell him ...' he hit me again across the mouth, '... that

when the boys ask for a donation ... we like to get it without any tricks.' He shoved his knee into my crotch and I screamed with pain as I lost consciousness.

I woke up lying on the bed with Farrell bending over me. 'They did you pretty good Harry.'

I couldn't talk through my swollen lips.

'Don't worry kid – you'll have a bodyguard from now on.'

He picked up the 'phone and dialled a number from a book he had produced.

'We'll cancel the next few dates Harry, tell them you're ill or something ...' He was dialling as he spoke. I heard him say to somebody at the other end: '... get to the American Embassy ... visa ... get the first plane ... soon as you can ... uh-huh ...'

I could only hear him through a blur. 'Don't worry Harry – it won't happen again – I've got a pal coming out to look after you – he's a cockney like us – a friend of mine—'

They issued a bulletin from the hotel which said that I was suffering from exhaustion. We cancelled two concerts but I hoped to be okay for the two we were doing at the weekend in Los Angeles.

I had been in bed for two days, a doctor found nothing was broken, all I needed was rest. I was given some pills that made me sleep the clock round. My mouth, except for a slight puffy look, felt all right and none of my teeth was broken.

I still ached all over, it was hard to believe anybody's frame could have stood up to what had happened. I had been kicked in the ribs, kneed in the crotch, I had bled profusely yet here I was all in one piece, a mass of bloody aches but all in one piece.

On the Friday morning Farrell brought my new body-

guard in. He was massive, looked like the one that is always
knocking Popeye about, he took my hand to shake it and
winced. 'Ooh sorry Harry,' he said. Farrell said, 'I don't
want you ever to let Mr Selfridge out of your sight – you
understand?' 'I understand Frank,' said the big one.

I smiled at him. 'What's your name?'

'Nipper Davis.'

'Nipper?'

'That's right Harry.' He grinned. 'If anybody ever gets
near you again, urchchch!' He made a gesture as if he
was wringing a towel out.

Newspapers all over the world had received the ex-
planatory bulletin. In no time writers were speculating
about what was wrong with me. To sell their sheets some
theorised that I had cancer, others talked of heart failure,
some suggested that I had spent too much time in the
sack with the opposite sex.

Flowers from kids all over the States were arriving. Farrell had them sent to various hospitals, making sure that
the photographers and columnists had been notified.

The announcement went out that I would be fit to play
Los Angeles on the Saturday night but till then I would
stay at the hotel in San Francisco.

It was on the Friday night my mother arrived.

She burst into the room like an uncontrolled kite.

'Where's my baby?' she asked, she had flown over the
Pole and looked like she had just come from a stall in
Bermondsey Market. 'I came as soon as I read about it.'

She brushed past all of them in the room, Farrell, Reg,
Nipper and Catgut.

'What he needs is a woman around here.' She glared
at the other fellows and sat down on the settee beside
me. I was half dressed, as she hugged me I winced with
pain.

'Don't worry son – mummy will look after you.'

'He's all right now Mrs Selfridge,' said Farrell.

'All right? All right?' she asked again. 'Look at him
he looks like a bloody ghost – how long is it since h
had any fresh air?'

Nobody spoke, we had all forgotten what fresh ai
was.

'If I had my way, I'd have him on the first aeroplan
out of here and back to London – you must have bee
working the poor little sod to death.' She crushed me t
her and I gasped. 'Look at him – don't worry Harry
mummy's here.'

For the first time she became aware of Reg standin
there. 'Couldn't you see what was happening to him?' sh
asked pointedly. 'Couldn't you have made them work hir
a bit less?'

Reg tried to speak.

'After all – you are his bloody father!'

I had to interrupt. 'Look mum, it's nothing to do witl
him or him or him or any of them – I just had a littl
mishap – now I'm okay so let's forget it – have you eater
would you like some food?'

She had another good look round and seemed to g
quieter. 'Yes I would as a matter of fact – I haven't eater
since I left London.'

Farrell was already on the 'phone dialling room service

'Are you pleased to see me Harry?'

' 'Course I am mum,' I said.

'You're really famous now you know – don't matte
where you go – in the pub – in the supermarket – or
the radio – it's all Harry Selfridge records.'

All the others had suddenly become interested. 'We've
got all your albums at home. Thank you for all the money
you've been sending me Harry.' She had now gone all sof
and I found myself liking her a lot more than I had done

'How's Mr Benjamin?'

'I got rid of him, he got all big-headed and kept telling everybody he was your father.'

I saw Reg pretend not to hear, watched him pick up a menu from the sideboard and read it.

'You'll have to stay a few days,' I said.

'I'd like to Harry, it must be lovely to see America – can I stay with you please Harry?'

' 'Course you can, I'll get someone to show you around.' It was Farrell talking.

'I'll take you if you like.' It was Reg.

'Thank you,' she said quietly, she let her eyes dwell on Reg for a long time, then she looked back at me, gave me a big hug. I should have been riddled with pain, but I wasn't – I liked it.

We finished the tour in Los Angeles. Farrell thought it would be a good idea if we all got on a plane and went to Nassau in the Bahamas for a holiday.

He had rented a house that belonged to a pop singer named Joe Breezi. There was me, Reg, the old lady and Nipper Davis. Farrell was going to stay in L.A., and Catgut went back to San Francisco because he liked the scene here.

We landed at Nassau, walked through customs and immigration unheeded, somebody laid on a taxi at the airport which whisked us away to a large private house on Cable Beach.

Obviously there had been a briefing before we arrived. When we got to the gates of the house there were two uniformed security men with batons and guns in holsters.

The butler carried our bags to individual rooms which were furnished in exquisite taste, mainly in yellow and green. There was a staff of three who did the cooking and housework.

I wished Nipper had not been with us but Farrell had sent him to keep an eye on me. Not only was it dangerous for me without Nipper, but Farrell had already handed a great deal of money back for the concert dates I couldn't fulfil, and didn't want to do that again.

We spent our time sitting in the garden overlooking the beach. In the evening we wandered over to the Casino and played roulette. I lost five hundred dollars in five attempts to win on number thirteen.

The moment I stopped playing, up came number thirteen.

By now I had been recognised by the American tourists, so we made a quick exit to the waiting taxi and cruised slowly around the island.

The sea was calm, the full moon was making the palms look like silhouettes of giant negroes. We stopped by a beach and stood drinking in the beauty of the night.

'Bit like Battersea,' said the old lady.

I watched Reg slip his hand into hers, it was a romantic setting, you couldn't help but remember all those Dorothy Lamour films they showed on telly.

Nipper picked up some stones and began throwing them in the water. I had a great desire to be with Eileen Dutton.

'Come on break it up – we're going,' I said.

We piled into the auto and drove home, as soon as we arrived I went straight up to my room and dialled the operator on the green 'phone by my bed. I gave her Eileen's number, two minutes later I was talking to her.

'Who is it?'

'It's me, Harry.'

'Harry? What time is it?'

'It's ten o'clock here, it must be three in the morning there.'

156

'Are you all right Harry?' She was awake now.

'I'm sorry to get you at this hour but I keep getting snubbed when I call you at the office.'

'Are you surprised?' she asked.

'You don't take notice of all you read in the papers do you Eileen?'

'Well – I believe what I see.'

'They make it up – look, don't let's talk about that – let's talk about us – Eileen I want to marry you.'

'You want to ...'

'That's if you'll have me.'

'Are you drunk Harry?'

'Eileen – I'm in a place called Nassau – outside there's a calm sea and a big moon and I wish I was sharing it with you – why don't you come out here?'

'I can't do that.'

'Why not – there's a plane which leaves daily from London and it gets here in nine hours – you could have a long weekend, please, please, Eileen.'

'I couldn't come all that way for a – what – a week-end!' She was saying no but I could feel she was thinking about it.

'Listen, the planes are empty at this time of year – get a plane ticket at London Airport tomorrow morning – I'll give you the money for the ticket when you get here – there's no need to book a hotel room, we've got a big house here – please come, you'll love it.'

I worked on her for four or five minutes more and although she wouldn't come the following day she agreed to come the day after. I hung up, put my swimming trunks on and rushed out towards the sea – gosh I felt good – the best I'd felt for weeks.

As I walked back to the house I tripped over Reg and the old lady cuddled up on the sandy beach.

I said, 'Why don't you two go to bed!' Which they did.

I played draughts with Nipper.

Frank Farrell made a deal for Harry Selfridge to appear for six weeks at the Green Baize, Las Vegas. The fee was one million dollars.

Farrell liked the idea of Las Vegas, it was where they really paid – big money.

As soon as the booking was announced, the seats went like wildfire. Farrell booked a plane and went there from L.A. to 'case it'.

A nine-seater air-conditioned Cadillac met him at the airport, the chauffeur pointed out the different casinos as they drove through the Strip.

Farrell had some picture at the back of his mind that one day he would be the owner of one of these.

Those small-time crooks at the Moor, at Pentonville and Parkhurst would surely be envious to hear that Frankie Farrell, a London villain, was now one of the big men out at Las Vegas. This was the big time, speak of Las Vegas and you thought of the greats – Al Capone, Bugsy Seigal, Nicky the Greek – this was the Big League. Play it sensibly and you could always be on the right side of the law too, that was the new way – the easy way. You own a casino with the percentages in your favour, you pay a bit to the Treasury and a bigger bit to yourself, it was a stupid dream but not too stupid, not when you had a property like Harry Selfridge.

The uniformed doorman rushed to the car door and opened it for Farrell. 'This way sir,' he beckoned.

He was led through a door that said 'Strictly Private', down a corridor to a heavily padded leather door that had no lock, no knocker just a bell-push, the doorman pushed this, a voice came over an unseen speaker, 'Who?'

'Mr Farrell has arrived sir,' said the doorman.

There was a pause, then a click, the door opened by itself and Farrell was looking at Alfred Camelia.

'Come in Mr Farrell,' Camelia said affably. 'This is a pleasure.' The door clicked shut behind them.

'Your boy with you?'

'No – he's having a little holiday – he's down in the Bahamas.'

'Good idea – good idea – keep him fresh – he's been setting the place alight here, there is hardly a seat left for him – he's a bigger seller than Presley y'know that? A bigger seller than Presley.' He repeated it as if he just couldn't believe it.

Farrell watched him as he tidied his desk with pale manicured hands. First the blotter, then the letter opener, then the desk clock then several pens.

'I heard he made a big impression,' said Farrell.

There was something that fascinated him about Alfred Camelia, word had it that he was the king of a multi-million empire in Las Vegas alone. Apart from the casino, he handled the call girl racket, narcotics and was boss of all the unions that kept Las Vegas ticking over as a twenty-four hour city.

'Big impression? We don't get that kind of reaction for Sinatra, Dean Martin and Sammy Davis all put together.'

His blue shirt and blue tie were immaculate, his silver grey suit looked like it had never been sat down in.

He began to tidy his desk again, shifting everything one inch over to the left.

'I wondered if you might consider selling a little part of him.'

Farrell felt all his reflexes come to life. 'I hadn't thought of it – no.'

'I could make you an attractive offer Frank, for a part or all of his contract – ever thought of retiring?'

Farrell's mind went back to the day he conned Solly Segal out of his deserts. He wondered whether Camelia might have something similar in mind. Farrell felt on good ground. The contract was lodged in a safe deposit box in Regent Street, London. Without that piece of paper nobody, nowhere, could do a thing with Harry Selfridge, but he wanted to hear what Camelia had in mind.

'We did a little research on you Frank, before you came here – we know your record – we know that you got that contract in a nice legal way.' He smiled a full smile at Farrell as he said it, '. . . some say you paid about two hundred thousand dollars for it.'

Farrell shifted as Camelia began to move everything over to the right again. 'I thought you might be interested in selling a half share, third share, anything so that when Harry comes back to Las Vegas again he comes to the Green Baize, what we call a goodwill contract.'

'I'll have to think about it.'

'All the time in the world Frank – there's a suite laid on for you – if you want any chips just sign for them, any broads or booze or anything, just ask Frank, it's on the house.'

'Thank you.'

'No – thank you Frank – thank you and Harry – have a good stay.' He led him to the door which in some mysterious way opened again by itself. The doorman was waiting outside with his hat in his hand. 'This way sir,' he said.

Farrell had a criminal's intuition that he was being set up for something, but he shrugged it off. Las Vegas was now legit and even if it wasn't he had Harry, he had a contract and he had plane tickets should he ever have to leave in a hurry.

Camelia walked back to his desk and once more shifted the blotter, the letter opener, the desk clock and pens. He turned, looked at himself in a wall mirror, smoothed his grey temples, flicked a speck from his tie then talked to his reflection as if it was another person.

'Alfredo,' he said, '... it will be like taking candy from a bambino.'

When she walked from the plane at Nassau International airport I suddenly realised what those kids who came to welcome me or wave goodbye went through.

I got a fleeting glimpse of her as she came down the plane steps, she boarded a bus and I didn't see her again till she got through customs. Luckily she had an up-to-date passport and no visas were necessary for Nassau so she was soon out.

She was dressed too warmly for the eighty-four degrees temperature, but she looked great. I took her weekend bag and threw it in the back of the car. We had it to ourselves, Nipper Davis was following in a taxi, there was no other way of getting rid of him. We went into a clinch and didn't break till she had to come up for air.

She was wide-eyed at the scenery and smell of bougain-villea in the air, the driver had a local station on the car radio, a steel band was playing 'Yellowbird', it was perfect. We were going to have a great couple of days.

That evening, after I had introduced her to Reg, the old lady, Nipper and the staff, we found we had been discreetly left to ourselves. I think the old lady had something to do with it.

The table was set, the lights were dimmed, the candles were lit and somebody had put a record of Neilson on the hi-fi, we were alone for the very first time in the ten months since we had first met.

We were served some local conch, followed by hot lobster, with some cold Chablis, strawberries to follow and coffee. Then the doors of the dining room were closed and we sat looking at each other, we just sat there half-smiling.

'I love you Eileen.'

She smiled wider and picked one of the hibiscus from a silver dish in the table centre. 'I'll bet you say that to all the girls,' she chided.

I took the bait and said, 'No I don't.'

She twisted the pink flower then said, 'There isn't a day gone by when I haven't thought about you.'

'Or me.' It was corny dialogue but to both of us in that setting, they were all the words we could find.

'Will you marry me Eileen?'

'I think you're very lovely Harry – that's why I'm here with you – but I don't know if it will work.'

'Why not?'

She wrinkled her brow as she tried to find the right words. 'Harry, you are – well – you're what you are – girls fall over themselves to get just a peep at you – if they thought you had a wife they'd – well I don't know what they'd do to you but they'd hate me – I'd get torn to pieces – you have a lot going for you Harry – you're still only twenty-two – why not wait a bit – anyway I'm up to my neck in Operation Dairy at present – I wouldn't be able to give you my undivided attention.'

It made sense. 'You won't run off with anybody else though – will you Eileen?'

'I promise.'

I took her hand and we stayed loving each other with looks, then the maid entered quietly and took the plates away. 'Did you enjoy it boss?' she asked.

'Beautiful,' I said. I was looking at Eileen.

Eileen travelled back with the old lady to London, they had become quite good pals.

163

When I arrived in Las Vegas, Farrell was waiting in this enormous Cadillac, he had already been there a week, he was pale and had a debauched look. I had a feeling he'd been playing it too often with the chicks there. I was surprised to hear him tell me he had been playing poker at night, usually into the early hours of the morning.

'I'm surprised you play poker.'

'It's the best game, you go in with a chance, the poker machines, blackjack, craps are all backed with percentages in favour of the house, with poker you have an even chance. I'll give you another surprise, you read that Vegas is full of smart guys – do you know how much I am up on the week?'

I shook my head.

'Fifteen thousand bucks – fifteen thousand! – that's a lotta potatoes.' Frank had rapidly picked up the jargon of the gambling fraternity.

We drove along and he pointed out the different casinos, who was appearing there, how much they were getting. 'See that place over there – they paid Tom Jones one hundred and eight-five grand for a week – a hundred and eight-five thousand bucks!'

'That's a lotta potatoes,' I said.

'You bet it's a lotta potatoes,' he replied. He either hadn't registered my sarcasm or else he had decided to ignore it.

On the opening night the place was jammed, it was a sell-out with some customers paying the head waiter as much as five hundred dollars for a table for four.

They were a great audience too. I expected to find a tough bunch of gamblers with dead pan faces and cigars stuck in the sides of their mouths, but the audience apart from a few celebrities were made up of middle-aged women with blue rinsed hair, young girls in party dresses and all-American boys.

They applauded generously and laughed at my jokes. In fact they were a better audience than we'd had on the tour, the hall was more intimate, the lighting was better and the band backing me had a roar when I needed it. Catgut conducted behind me and when I did the quiet numbers he produced his guitar.

Between numbers I talked, my Cockney accent seemed out of place but they seemed to understand me.

'I've been told how to leave Las Vegas with a small fortune,' I confided to the audience, '... arrive with a large one!' They all clapped that one.

'I've been told how to save money here – when you get off the aeroplane at Las Vegas Airport – walk straight into the propeller.'

These lines had been written for me by a gag writer before we left L.A. I was amazed at the reaction they got, I felt like another Bob Hope. With each performance I added more and more of this patter, and was getting a reputation for being quite a wit. I threw quite a few original ideas in and found they were getting bigger laughs than the ones the writer had written for me.

I had crowds of people come into the dressing-room after each performance, there was lots of booze and food available served by two waiters for each and every one to enjoy.

On the third night in came Connie Parnell, an American television star who was one of the most beautiful young ladies in the USA. She was blonde, blue-eyed, a figure like the Venus de Milo and almost every male in America was dying to make it with her.

The flash bulbs popped like firecrackers as the press boys took us kissing and hugging each other, she came to the show four nights in a row, and on the fourth night it was all over Las Vegas that she had spent each day and night in my suite. That weekend the world press reported that Connie Parnell, the twenty-six year old star of television was madly in love with Harry Selfridge, a twenty-two year old milkman turned pop singer.

Disc jockeys shouted it from the radio sets and invariably followed it up by playing a record of Fats Waller singing, 'My very good friend, the milkman says . . .'

The truth was I really didn't mind Connie being there, she was good fun, and helped to break the boredom of Las Vegas, which certainly was a boring place to be if you were not a gambler, but I wasn't in love with her. She was enjoying the fantastic worldwide coverage our supposed romance was getting, but she was a bit too brassy for me. I mean, I know I'm not from the blue-blooded stock but put Connie alongside Eileen and it was like putting a dray horse against Nijinsky.

The bloody awful part about it was, Eileen had stopped taking my 'phone calls again. I sent a four page telegram but she ignored that too.

I was becoming more and more disillusioned with this star tag, I honestly wished I was a milkman again.

The poker school was never in the main betting section, they played in small ante-rooms with just a waiter in discreet attendance.

The gamblers were out of towners, sometimes from L.A., some came from Chicago and quite a few flew up from Texas in private jets.

Farrell had a reputation by now. He was reckoned to be a good poker player – an impassive face – no nervous twitch, no finger drumming. Just a dead pan that gave nothing away.

He had played a lot of poker during his years inside, he'd had lot of practice watching other prisoners' reactions, raising and lowering, true it had only been for a cigarette or a ration of soap, but it was as important then as the thirty thousand dollars he was winning since he'd started playing in Las Vegas.

The quiet room with the shaded light above a green baize table was as quiet as a tomb, only an occasional word of, 'raise' or, 'call' and the intermittent click of five hundred dollar chips broke the silence.

Farrell looked across at the other players, there was a scrap dealer from San Francisco, a man that had a greyhound track somewhere in Houston and a fellow who didn't have much to say from Seattle. They were all about Farrell's age give or take a couple of years.

The scrap dealer and the Texan seemed pretty open but Farrell wasn't too sure about the guy from Seattle, his name was Al Gold and each time Farrell looked at him he looked like the Sphinx.

Farrell made a quick appraisal of the game so far, the stakes were the highest he had ever played for, five hundred dollar minimum and no limit.

He had already dropped twenty thousand dollars and they'd only been playing an hour. He wasn't too worried, some of his big wins had come only an hour or so before they called it a day which sometimes was after seven a.m.

Every time Farrell had a good hand Gold threw in, he asked for a new pack of cards but it made no difference to his luck, he signed a chit for another fifty thousand dollars worth of chips, in another hour they had dwindled, the scrap dealer and greyhound track man backed out and were watching them. Farrell and Gold began to go for really high pots.

Farrell had a little run of good luck and recouped ten thousand of his losses but he was still eighty thousand down.

'Do you want to call it a day?' asked Gold quietly.

Farrell knew his nerves were beginning to show. Gold was as cool as they come. On the spur of the moment

167

Farrell said, 'No – I'll take one hundred thousand dollars more and we'll double the stakes.'

'Just as you wish Mr Farrell,' said Gold.

Farrell took a quick look behind his shoulder to see if anybody could be tipping-off Gold on his hand. He looked casually at the ceiling and asked for a new set of cards, he studied the backs to see if he could detect a mark but they were absolutely plain. He seemed to be losing too heavily, his luck must return soon – it had to, he reckoned he was as good a poker player as Gold, but so far the cards hadn't come up for him. If he lost this next stint he would be two hundred thousand dollars down, it was about all he had – good thing he had Harry.

'Hi, Frank!' It was Alfred Camelia speaking on the 'phone. 'Long session last night huh?'

'Yeah,' said Farrell. 'Long session.' He had been awake only ten minutes. It was three in the afternoon.

'Four hundred and fifty thousand dollars you dropped – that's a lotta mazoola.'

'Was it four hundred and fifty thousand?'

'I've got your chits in front of me here, four hundred and fifty thousand. Why didn't you call it a day? You can't take that sort of loss – that Al Gold is one of the best poker players in the world – weren't you told that?'

He had been warned, what nobody had told him was that he had been allowed to win over the past two weeks by fellows who threw in or knew he had a better hand, they had been picked by Camelia to let him win over and over again until he was happy that he was the best player in the casino.

That's when Camelia brought in Al Gold from Seattle, for a five thousand dollar fee Gold had been instructed to push Farrell as far as he could, the result was that

Farrell now owed the casino four hundred and fifty thousand dollars. It wasn't hard to lose that amount when you are against the world's best poker player, not for the stakes Farrell had called.

'Yeah. I was warned,' sighed Farrell into the 'phone.

'How do we get paid Frank?'

'Don't worry I'll pay you.'

'I'm not worried Frank. You know there's tax to pay on your boy's earnings, there's various bills you have to pay for entertaining here – in all – it's half a million dollars.'

'Yeah I know.' The magnitude of that amount was beginning to dawn on him.

'Come down and see me when you are dressed huh?'

'Okay – I'll be down.'

When Farrell was shaved and showered he felt a little more relieved. At first he had been a bit frightened, he was not in the kindergarten – he was in the big league, these casino bosses had been very friendly towards him, why shouldn't they be – Harry was doing great business for them, he had engineered some great publicity for the Green Baize by linking Connie Parnell and Harry, and he could pay the half million dollars if not now – in future engagements.

Camelia was waiting in his office with his lawyer and an aide he introduced as Big Jim Smith, they shook hands all round then sat down.

Camelia began to adjust the top of his desk.

'Frank – I was just telling the gentlemen you dropped nearly half a million bucks last night.'

'That's right,' said Farrell. Big Jim whistled, the lawyer Lon Gotlieb shook his head.

'That's a lotta bread,' said Smith.

'A lotta bread,' said Gotlieb.

'I'm a gambling man myself Frank,' said Camelia, 'but I only bet on even chances – I'd cut the cards with any-

169

body – I'd roll a dice for the highest number or I'd toss a coin – that's fair odds isn't it Frank?'

'You couldn't get fairer,' said Farrell.

'Feel lucky Frank?'

'How d'ye mean?'

'Double or quits?'

'For a million dollars!?' gasped Farrell.

'Tell you what I'll do – toss a coin Frank, if you win – you owe me nothing – if you lose – you let Harry continue here for six more weeks.'

'I don't think he wants to do another six weeks, he's had enough of Las Vegas.'

'You are his manager Frank – make him – we'll announce that owing to public demand, Harry is going to do six more weeks at the Green Baize – it means a half million dollars to you, plus the commission you're gonna pick up on his further one million.'

'I'll have to talk to him first,' said Farrell.

'Look Frank, I am making you a great offer, there is no way you can lose. Tell your boy the contract has been extended for another six weeks – tell him we had options, you're not doing this for chicken feed – in actual – you are getting one and a half million dollars – now then extend the contract or pay me on these IOUs – it's up to you.'

Farrell looked at the three pairs of eyes demanding his answer.

'All right – double or quits.'

'What do you want to do, cut for it or toss for it? Which?'

'I'll cut.'

Camelia produced a wrapped deck of cards, he broke the seal and handed them to Farrell for inspection. 'Shuffle them.'

Farrell shuffled the pack half a dozen times and laid them on the desk.

'Would you like to cut first Frank?'

'No, go ahead.'

Camelia made his cut, then turned it face upwards – the three of diamonds.

Farrell felt the charge as he reached, the chances on a quick calculation were over forty to one in his favour – he cut – the deuce of spades.

There was a moment's silence then Camelia said to Big Jim, 'Tell the press office to announce that Harry Selfridge is being held over for a further six weeks.' He turned to Farrell and said, 'Now Frank if you will excuse me – I have some business.'

When Farrell got into the corridor he didn't know whether he had been set up or not.

He felt relieved he was off the hook for a half million dollars.

'What do you mean another six weeks – who said so?'

'They want you to do six more weeks, it's a great compliment,' glared Farrell.

'Look Frank, when I signed the contract, I read it, there was no further six weeks agreed on.'

'What's wrong with earning another million dollars?'

'I don't want a million dollars, I want to go some place where I can go for a walk and not be mobbed. I want to get some fresh air, be a human being again. This is not the life I want – four bloody walls day in day out – Christ, I'm twenty-two – I want to start living again – when I finish on Saturday night I'm going back to England.'

'You bloody well go back to England, you'll have to pay tax on all your earnings, everything from the day you started, they'll claim ninety-eight per cent from you.'

'Well I'll bloody well pay it – I was bloody happy then, I'm not bloody happy now – my bloody life has come to a standstill.'

'You can't go back to England.'

'Why not?' I shouted.

'Because I've given my word.'

'*Your* bloody word – don't *I* count? Didn't anybody think of asking me – what *am* I for Chrissake?'

'Please Harry do it for me.'

'For you? Haven't you had enough? Booze, broads, gambling, luxury travel, Christ Farrell you've had more than enough – I want to be on a plane to London on Sunday morning. You tell whoever you have to tell, that as my contract states I'm finished from Saturday. I'm going to take a few months off and then . . .'

I didn't see it coming, Farrell hit me with the back of his hand, I saw stars, blood was coming from my nose and mouth.

'You'll do as *I* say,' he shouted. 'I've had enough shit from you – do as I say or you'll wish you'd never been born.' He reached for the door and slammed it as he went red-faced down the corridor.

I sat down on the settee and watched the blood drip onto my white slacks.

I must have sat there for three or four minutes, when Reg walked into the room.

'Blimey, Harry what've you done?'

'I walked into a right hander.'

He went into the bathroom, and soaked a hand towel with cold water which he pressed gently on my mouth.

'Farrell do it Harry?'

I nodded.

'I told you to be careful didn't I, son?'

I found it hard to talk – I nodded again. I was crying not with pain – I felt so – I suppose humiliated is the word.

'The bastard,' hissed Reg.

I sat there for two more minutes then said, 'I'd like you to do something for me Reg – nip down to Pan Am and book a ticket in the name of Charlie something or other on the first flight to London on Sunday morning. Don't tell a soul, I've had enough of this lark, I'm going home.'

'They've announced you're here for six more weeks Harry.'

'I know – well if they want me they can come and get me can't they.'

'Watch it Harry – these people aren't boy scouts y'know.'

'Look Reg, I belong to these people while I'm a performer earning thousands – if I make an announcement that I'm giving up show business they can't own me can they, 'cos there'll be no bloody money coming in.'

'You sure that's what you want Harry?'

'Yes Reg – it's exactly what I want.'

'Okay Harry, I'll do as you say.'

Reg went off. I'd made up my mind I was going to have just twenty-four more hours in show business. Suddenly my mouth didn't hurt, I felt good, I was going home.

Big Jim Smith hit Farrell again. Farrell had tried fighting back but knew enough about the game to realise he was outclassed. Alone in his room, Smith and another gorilla had walked in and almost knocked him senseless.

'You'd better have an answer by the time Camelia gets here!' He hit Farrell again and gave the okay for the other guy to let go, he had been holding Farrell's arms behind him while Smith waded in.

Smith watched him sink to the carpet, he then picked up the house 'phone and called Alfred Camelia.

'I think he's ready now Mr Camelia.'

The two of them hoisted Farrell into a deep armchair, Smith walked into the bathroom and filled a glass with ice cold drinking water. When he came back he threw it in Farrell's face.

Camelia entered the room and looked at Farrell.

'Where is he? Where is Selfridge?'

'I don't know – I really don't know.'

'I've got two thousand people out in that theatre waiting for him to walk on and do his goddam act – now where is he?'

'Want me to work him over a little more boss?' asked Smith.

Before either of them could decide, the 'phone rang. Big Jim picked it up. 'Yeah, he's here – it's for you boss.'

Camelia picked up the 'phone, 'Camelia.' He listened for almost a minute, his eyes getting darker. He quietly replaced the receiver.

'Your boy was seen getting on a plane in Los Angeles for London,' he said slowly to Farrell. 'I gave you a great opportunity to redeem your loan to us, this isn't exactly the act of an English gentleman is it Frank? Letting your boy welsh on a contract – there's another six weeks to play.'

He knelt down beside Farrell. 'Listen punk – don't come to Las Vegas trying to make a monkey of people like me – maybe it works with your little Soho gangs but not out here with top bananas – you are small fry – get that – you are nothing. Now listen to what I am going to say – listen good because if you don't they are going to find your remains in a hundred years somewhere out in that Nevada desert – planted good and deep – understand?'

Farrell nodded his head, he couldn't have formed words if he tried.

'I am sending Smith and Garcia here to London with you – you can be there in twelve hours from now. I want you to find Selfridge and bring him back in forty-eight hours – understand? We'll make an announcement that he has been taken ill – but I want him in this building ready to perform by Tuesday night – are you with me?'

There was a knock at the door, Garcia stepped behind it as it opened, in walked Nipper Davis.

'Seen Harry, Mr Farrell?' he blurted. He took in Farrell's mangled features, was about to say something when Garcia karate chopped him from behind, he fell like a landslide.

'Be ready to leave in half an hour Farrell,' said Smith.

As Garcia, Big Jim Smith and Camelia left the suite that had belonged to Harry, Nipper came to, he looked around dazedly and said, 'What happened Mr Farrell?'

Farrell picked up the telephone at his elbow, the whole instrument, and smashed it down on Nipper's head. Nipper went back to his peaceful world.

I was in a deep sleep after the flight from Los Angeles. Somehow I had got from door to door with very few people recognising me – I didn't have a bag or suitcase – I had left just as I was. I had made good connections at the airport and was sleeping like a babe, it was the 'phone that woke me.

For a minute I had to figure what city in what part of the world I was in. Slowly the last dozen hours or so came back to me.

'Hello?' It was the overseas operator asking if I could take a personal call – I half expected to hear Farrell's voice but it was Reg.

'Harry?'

'Yes, Reg.'

'Look mate, I've been trying to get you for an hour, listen to me kid – Farrell has left Las Vegas with two of Camelia's strong arm boys and they've got instructions not to come back without you. Harry, they mean business, they could be arriving soon, now you do what you like, but they're mean bastards so I'm ringing you to be prepared, y'understand?'

'Yes Reg, I understand.'

'Get some protection – see the police or somebody but don't let them get you alone, okay?'

'Okay Reg – I'll think of something.'

'Ta-ta kid – look after yourself now.'

'Righto Reg.'

He hung up.

I looked at my watch, it was almost eight o'clock on a

Monday morning. I dressed quickly and left the apartment. I had no idea where to go, then suddenly I had a thought. I stopped a cab and gave him the address of Dutton's Dairy in Battersea.

When I arrived, the place was almost empty, most of the milkmen were on their rounds. Eileen had not arrived. I did a quick exit and went back over the bridge again. I saw a Dutton's milk float, recognised a milkman named Sammy who I knew vaguely.

'Where's Jim Lloyd?'

'Hello Harry,' he said, all surprised. 'How are you?'

'I'm fine – where's Jim?' I asked again.

'Jim? He's taken the week off – he's at home as far as I know.'

'He's still at Meadow Road isn't he?'

'Far as I know Harry.'

I dashed off and managed to get a taxi cruising along the Embankment – I gave him the Meadow Road address.

'Hello Harry!' Jim said, his face lighting up. 'What are you doing ...'

Before he could say anything more, I pushed him inside. 'Jim, I need your help.'

'What's wrong kid?'

I told him, the whole story. When I'd finished, he sat quiet for a while. Then he stood up and said, 'You've been getting in some fair old scrapes haven't you mate.'

There was a Mercedes saloon with black windows waiting for Smith, Garcia and Farrell at London Heathrow.

Farrell was wearing dark glasses to hide the puffed, black eyes he had got back in Las Vegas. It was when the driver handed the Americans a Smith and Wesson each that he realised they had been travelling without guns, he had been hoping that security checks would have unearthed them, had they been found and apprehended he was going to make a run for it, but it seemed his luck was running out. First his big loss at poker, then the deuce he turned up on the cut, losing Harry and now sitting between two Mafia type guardians who would think no more of killing him than of blowing their noses.

'Where do we go?'

'We'll try his flat first, it's at the beginning of Edgware Road.'

'If he's not there, where?' asked Smith.

Farrell looked at his watch, it was nine forty-five.

'Well – it's morning – we could try my office – he may have called there.'

'Let's hope so for your sake,' said Garcia.

They pulled up outside the block where Harry had an apartment. Farrell had been there once and knew the flat.

He rang the bell and waited, there was no reply.

'Try it again,' said Smith. Again no reply.

'Step aside,' said Smith. He produced the gun and emptied three chambers into the lock, he kicked the door open. Smith entered, gun in hand, searching, he pulled open cupboards, looked under the slept-in bed, when he was satisfied the flat was empty he turned to Farrell. 'Okay – your office next.'

They walked out of the building into the waiting car – not a soul appeared to have heard the gunshots or, if they had, they were not going to interfere.

The next stop was Farrell's office in Bond Street.

Solly Segal had just put a new blotter into the pad, he looked surprised when the three of them walked in.

'Seen Harry?' asked Farrell.

'Harry? Harry?' He looked at Farrell as if he was mad. 'Harry's in Las Vegas.'

'He left last night – thought he might have been here.'

'No he hasn't been here.'

'What's his mother's address?'

'What do you want his mother's address ...'

'Stop asking fucking questions – where does his mother live?'

'I don't know.'

Smith leaned over the desk and said, 'Listen bright eyes – I want his mother's address – and any other address Harry Selfridge is likely to be.'

Solly didn't like any of this trio, he intended to let them know.

'Well – you can't have them.'

Smith looked at Garcia, who walked to the door and closed it quietly. As he walked back he was slipping on some brass knuckledusters.

Smith took a pad and pencil, 'Write down any of the addresses where you think Selfridge might be.'

Solly could not take his eyes off Garcia as he began to punch his other hand with the knuckledusters. One thing Solly was sure he could not take was physical pain, as Garcia walked towards him he grabbed the pad and wrote down Harry's mother's address, then Jim Lloyd's, as an afterthought he added the road that Dutton's Dairies was in.

'You sure this is all?' asked Smith.

'It's all, I swear,' said Solly.

As the three left, Solly made for the toilet and was violently ill.

I was at Jim's, up in the bathroom. The kids had left for school a quarter of an hour before. I'd heard them laughing as they got in the car Jim had bought Daphne as a birthday present. Up the stairs wafted the appetising aroma of eggs and bacon Jim was cooking for us – as I walked into the kitchen he was setting the table.

'Soon be ready kid – have a good shower?' he asked.

I was about to answer when I saw the Mercedes grind to a halt outside Jim's front gate. When I saw Farrell step out and look for the number, I shouted to Jim, 'It's them!'

He dropped the egg slice he was about to turn the bacon with and said, 'Down the garden – over the wall – go to the dairy – I'll pick you up there later!'

I pushed open the double doors to the garden, scaled the wall at the bottom and ran down the street towards the main road – in the distance I saw a bus coming. I raced it to the stop, then jumped aboard, the conductress almost had a fit. 'Blimey it's Harry Selfridge!' I gave her a pound note, 'Albert Bridge – please.'

'That's all right Harry,' she said as she patted her hair. 'Have this on the London Passenger Transport Board.' She gave me my pound back again. 'God knows who needs it most,' I gagged. 'Hark at bleedin' Paul Getty,' she laughed as she rang the bell for the bus to go.

Jim Lloyd answered the door to Farrell's knock, he looked questioningly at the trio as they waited for an answer to Farrell's 'Is Harry here?'

'No he's not,' said Jim.

'Mind if we take a look?' asked Farrell.

' 'Course I mind.' Jim blocked the doorway to stop any intrusion.

'Step aside or I'll blow your goddam head off your shoulders.' It was Big Jim Smith speaking as he produced the Smith and Wesson from his top coat pocket.

Jim couldn't believe what he was seeing, this was Meadow Road, the most exciting thing that had happened in this road prior to Jim and Harry appearing on television was when somebody had jacked up a Ford Prefect outside a neighbour's house one night and stolen one of the back wheels. Now here he was looking down the barrel of a revolver held by somebody who certainly wasn't trying to make an impression.

The three of them pushed past Jim and entered the living room. 'Look upstairs Farrell,' ordered Smith. Garcia walked to the toilet and Big Jim went to the kitchen, he turned to Jim now standing in the living room. 'Who else is here?'

'Nobody,' said Jim.

'Do you always eat two breakfasts?'

Jim looked at the two places he had set, then to the large pan of eggs and sizzling bacon.

'Where is he?' demanded Smith.

'I don't know!'

Crash! Smith's gun smashed against the side of Jim's head, he fell dazed. 'Pick him up, put him in the car! What's the next address?'

'Dutton's Dairies – it's where he used to work.'

'Okay let's go – I don't know if you remember what Camelia said but he wants Harry Selfridge back in Vegas in forty-eight hours – now come on – move it!'

They pulled Jim Lloyd to his feet and took him out to the Mercedes.

At that moment Mrs Adams, a neighbour of Jim's was passing. She saw the two men holding Jim between them, she stopped. 'You all right Mr Lloyd?' she asked concerned.

'Get to hell out of it,' snapped Smith as they crammed into the Mercedes.

Mrs Adams watched the car disappear, then entered her own gate. When she told old Mr Adams, her husband for forty-two years, he decided to 'phone the police.

The calls were assembled at New Scotland Yard, the young police sergeant was describing the incidents to his superior, Inspector Grant.

'The first call sir, was that three men had entered the Edgware Road apartments and blown the lock off with three revolver shots; the second was from a theatrical agent in Bond Street who said that three men, two with American accents, had forced him to give them the addresses where Harry Selfridge might be; ten minutes ago we had a call from a Mr Adams who said his wife had seen three men leaving with a Jim Lloyd – he was once Harry Selfridge's partner – he looked as if he had been hit. They got into a dark blue car with black windows – she didn't know the make because she doesn't recognise cars from their makes and her eyes weren't good enough to take the number, but somebody else at the Edgware Road flats thinks it was a Mercedes.'

Inspector Grant made a quick decision. 'Get a call out to South Division, look for a car with black windows – arrest any suspects.'

'Sir, it seems they have guns.'

'Ummm, I don't think I can issue guns.'

'What if they start shooting sir?' asked the sergeant.

'Yes – er – um – tell them to use their truncheons.'

'Truncheons? Is that all sir?'

'Yes sergeant.'

'Yes sir.' The sergeant raised his eyes to the ceiling and made for the door, as he closed it, he muttered, 'The bloody Mafia's here and we can use our truncheons – how jolly!'

I arrived at Dutton's. Why, I didn't know. On reflection I'd have been better off getting on a train to Scotland or North Wales or anywhere, why I was taking my problems to the dairy was a bit of a liberty, but in truth I needed a few friendly faces, I could find those amongst my old mates.

'Hello Harry boy – come for your old job back?' they laughed as I walked into the yard.

I waved and chatted to some of them, then walked into the office. Eileen was there, she looked great.

'Hello Harry – what a surprise,' she said.

'Yes, I ran out of milk in Las Vegas,' I laughed.

We both stood awkwardly.

'Can I get you anything?'

'No,' I said. 'I just popped in to see if you'd marry me.'

She laughed, 'You're always making jokes Harry.'

'I'm not joking Eileen – I'm serious – I'm not staying in show business – I've given it up – I gave it up yesterday – I'm not going back to it again – ever.'

'Harry are you really serious?'

'I'm really serious.'

'Yesterday? You mean you could leave people like Farrell and all those friendly types we keep reading about every day of the week.' She searched my face for the answer.

'I wouldn't mind starting where I left off – as a milkman.'

'Harry Selfridge, I know you've been paying money into our bank to keep us going . . .'

I was about to lie my way out of it but she went on : '. . . it was marvellous of you – now we're on our feet again, we're doing well and I intend to repay every penny to you Harry – but I don't think I could marry you Harry – you'd have to show me you were through with that crowd of degenerates you have been running around with . . .'

The door burst open, in stumbled Jim Lloyd, his face had dried blood on. He was still in his shirtsleeves. Eileen gave a stifled scream. In walked Farrell followed by two faces I recognised from the Green Baize in Las Vegas.

'Hello Harry,' said Farrell. 'We've been looking for you halfway round the world.'

'I told you I was leaving Farrell, what you are doing

183

here I don't know, I'm through with show business – it's as simple as that.'

'Alfred Camelia has different ideas about that Mr Selfridge,' said the heavier of the other two.

Farrell jerked his head towards the last speaker – 'That's Big Jim Smith and that's Mr Garcia – they've been sent to chaperon you back to Las Vegas – we can get a plane right away. We can be back in Nevada in time for Tuesday's performances, you've already missed Sunday and Monday Harry, we can't stall the audiences too long – as you know Mr Camelia will be losing a lot of custom.'

'I'm not interested in Mr Camelia, Frank – I told you I'm through.'

'Will you hooligans leave this office at once.' It was Eileen speaking, flushed and angry.

'Shut the dame up.' The one named Smith was speaking to Garcia.

Garcia walked towards Eileen and said, 'Cool it – let the men talk.'

'How dare you,' said Eileen, she picked up the 'phone and began to dial. 'I told you to shut the dame up,' roared Smith. Garcia took the 'phone from Eileen's hand, as she looked at him in disbelief he slapped her with the flat of his open hand across the cheek. 'Now behave lady,' he said quietly. None of us moved.

She stared at him, then Farrell, then Smith, then me – for a long time she stared at me, then she began to sob.

'Here's what we're gonna do Harry – Farrell and you and me are going back to Vegas.' Smith was looking at me to make sure I understood what he was saying, he was enunciating every word. 'Garcia here will look after the dame, when we have arrived in Las Vegas, without any bother, your lady friend will be allowed to leave. If we don't get back the way we planned – Little Miss Muffet here will not wake up to see tomorrow again – do I make myself clear?'

I looked at Jim Lloyd who was watching every one of us in turn. 'You'd better do as they say Harry,' his eyes were telling me, he didn't speak but I knew what he was trying to say. It seemed I had caused enough distress for one day. I made up my mind to go back with them the way Smith had planned.

'Okay,' I said. 'I'll do as you say – there's one thing though—' I turned to Garcia. 'You harm one hair of her head and I'll kill you personally.' I turned and left the office.

I walked to the end of the yard towards the Mercedes, Jim Lloyd came running after me. 'Harry!' he shouted. 'Harry!'

I stopped and turned, he came running up, Smith and Farrell walked towards their car. 'I'm sorry about all this kid.'

'It's not your fault Jim.' As I was speaking I saw one of the milk floats coming up the street, it had a few full crates on but mostly empties, it tooted to the Mercedes to move forward so as it could enter the yard. I saw an opportunity to get out of this mess. As the chauffeur climbed in to ease the saloon forward I took Jim's hand to shake it, over the noise of the engine starting, I said to Jim, 'Get back there and look after that bastard Garcia – I'm going for a ride.' I saw Jim look wide-eyed as I jumped onto the milk float, I pushed Clarence the bird watcher off the seat and pressed the starter, as he fell to the floor with surprise I was away down the street doing a top speed of twenty miles an hour – it felt like I was standing still. Clarence's eyes were like organ stops as he hung on looking first at me then back at the Merc.

Farrell and Smith, realising what had happened, were telling the driver of the Mercedes to reverse and get after

185

me, luckily another milk float had arrived at the same time and slowed up the proceedings.

I saw the driver of the Merc in my mirror reverse about twenty yards and then drive smack into the other milk float to clear a way. It came towards me. I got on the crown of the narrow road to make sure it didn't pass me, then I drove out on to the Albert Bridge, it was clear. I kept to the middle of the lane to stop them overtaking.

Suddenly – bang! A milk bottle shattered by my ear. I looked in the mirror to see Smith with a revolver firing at me Chicago style from the back window of the saloon. Bang! there was another. Christ! This wasn't really happening was it? They were real bloody bullets coming my way – on the Albert Bridge – on a Monday morning – there was a gang of Mafia gangsters actually firing at me – me! Harry Selfridge from Battersea. I pushed the starter but the speed was governed. What the hell had made me try to make a getaway from a Mercedes on a bloody milk float? I saw the Merc stop to get a good run so as it could pass and hem me in, it was fifty yards back – seventy-five – a hundred – then I saw it begin to roar up to me.

Clarence saw it too, he shouted. 'Harry – I think some men in the car behind want a word with you!'

I shouted, 'Take the wheel Clarence!' We changed places, I reached into the crates and got a full bottle of milk and threw it in the path of the oncoming Merc, then another, then another, as fast as I could I threw them, they exploded like water bombs, thick glass covering the road.

A tyre exploded, I watched the Merc go into a wobble then crash into the balustrade of the bridge. The doors flew open with the impact, the windshield was smashed to smithereens. I could see the flashing blue light of the police car and the uniformed figures of policemen running towards the wreck with their truncheons drawn.

I looked at the advert in the local paper. 'The family dairy that serves the family – Dutton's and Company'. 'I like that ad,' I said. I was in the office with my feet up on the desk.

'Well there's one thing that's certain, it's a family business all right,' said Eileen. She smiled as the old lady put a cup of coffee on the desk for me. 'Thanks mum,' I said. 'If I wasn't married to this one I'd take you out tonight!'

'Ooh I don't think your father would like it – would you Reg?'

Reg was just outside in the yard. 'I don't mind him it's the others,' he laughed.

Jim poked his head in. 'Fancy coming up the club tomorrow night Harry?'

'Okay if the missus comes with me.' I put my arm round Eileen and gave her a big wet kiss.

Solly Segal got up from his desk and said, 'How the bloody hell you expect an accountant to keep books with all this sex going on around him is beyond me.'

HUMOUR

0352	Star	
300698	Woody Allen **GETTING EVEN**	50p*
398973	Alida Baxter **FLAT ON MY BACK**	50p
397187	**OUT ON MY EAR**	60p
397101	**UP TO MY NECK**	50p
398612	Alex Duncan **IT'S A VET'S LIFE**	60p
398795	**THE VET HAS NINE LIVES**	50p
395389	**VETS IN CONGRESS**	60p
396245	David Dawson **VET IN DOWNLAND**	60p
397535	Stephen John **WHAT A WAY TO GO!** (see also Tandem Humour)	50p
397314	King Kong **MY SIDE**	60p
396016	Andre Launay **COME INTO MY BED**	60p
397527	Jack Millmay **REVELATIONS FROM THE** **RAG TRADE**	50p
395907	Stanley Morgan **A BLOW FOR GABRIEL HORN**	70p
396237	**INSIDE ALBERT SHIFTY**	70p
398965	**RUSS TOBIN'S BEDSIDE GUIDE** **TO SMOOTHER SEDUCTION**	60p
397454	**THE FLY BOYS: SKY-JACKED**	60p
395591	**RUSS TOBIN'S¦:HARD UP**	70p
396954	Harry Secombe **GOON FOR LUNCH**	60p
39899X	Peter Vincent **THE TWO RONNIES: BUT FIRST** **THE NEWS**	60p
301082	**MORE OF THE TWO RONNIES:** **NICE TO BE WITH YOU AGAIN!**	60p
396148	Keith Waterhouse **MONDAYS, THURSDAYS (NF)**	60p

†For sale in Britain and Ireland only.
*Not for sale in Canada.

BIOGRAPHY

0352	Star

General (all are illustrated)

395680	Doris Day & A. E. Hotchner **DORIS DAY, HER OWN STORY**	95p *
396865	Margaret, Duchess of Argyll **FORGET NOT**	70p
398078	The Duchess of Bedford **NICOLE NOBODY**	75p
396091	Max Bygraves **I WANNA TELL YOU A STORY**	70p
397004	Tommy Cooper **JUST LIKE THAT!** (Large Format)	50p
39854X	Paul Dunn **THE OSMONDS**	80p*
397071	Margot Fonteyn **MARGOT FONTEYN**	75p
396601	Gerold Frank **JUDY** (Large Format)	£1.95p *
300299	Noele Gordon **MY LIFE AT CROSSROADS**	50p
39594X	Frankie Howerd **ON THE WAY I LOST IT**	85p
398108	Brian Johnston **IT'S BEEN A LOT OF FUN**	60p
396873	Renee Jordan **STREISAND**	75p
39644X	Hildegarde Knef **THE VERDICT**	95p
398841	Vera Lynn **VOCAL REFRAIN**	60p
396083	Lilli Palmer **CHANGE LOBSTERS AND DANCE**	95p
398396	Pat Phoenix **ALL MY BURNING BRIDGES**	60p
396806	Brian Rix **MY FARCE FROM MY ELBOW**	75p
398876	Charles Thompson **BING**	70p
395583	Tennessee Williams **MEMOIRS**	85p
397268	Mike and Bernie Winters **SHAKE A PAGODA TREE**	60p

†For sale in Britain and Ireland only.
*Not for sale in Canada.

GENERAL FICTION

0352   Star

396423	Mary Ann Ashe **RING OF ROSES**	**60p**
396938	Andre P. Brink **LOOKING ON DARKNESS**	**95p**
39613X	William Burroughs **DEAD FINGERS TALK**	**75p**
398663	Jackie Collins **THE WORLD IS FULL OF DIVORCED WOMEN**	**50p**
398752	**THE WORLD IS FULL OF MARRIED MEN**	**50p**
300671	Eric Corder **HELLBOTTOM**	**75p***
300086	**THE LONG TATTOO**	**40p***
398515	**RUNNING DOGS**	**60p***
396113	Robertson Davies **FIFTH BUSINESS**	**95p**
396857	Terry Fisher **IF YOU'VE GOT THE MONEY**	**70p**
39840X	Knight Isaacson **THE STORE**	**60p**
396105	Gavin Lambert **IN THE NIGHT ALL CATS ARE GREY**	**75p**
396334	**THE SLIDE AREA**	**75p**
398299	Robin Maugham **THE SIGN**	**55p***
397594	Clayton Moore **END OF RECKONING**	**60p***
397608	**141 TERRACE DRIVE**	**60p***
397543	**RIVER FALLS**	**60p***
397667	**SECRET FIRE**	**60p***
397659	**THE CORRUPTERS**	**60p***
397551	**WESLEY SHERIDAN**	**60p***
300809	Molly Parkin **LOVE ALL**	**50p**
397179	**UP TIGHT**	**60p**
396946	Judith Rossner **TO THE PRECIPICE**	**85p***

†For sale in Britain and Ireland only.
*Not for sale in Canada.

Wyndham Books are obtainable from many booksellers and newsagents. If you have any difficulty please send purchase price plus postage on the scale below to:

Wyndham Cash Sales
P.O. Box 11
Falmouth
Cornwall
OR
Star Book Service,
G.P.O. Box 29,
Douglas,
Isle of Man,
British Isles.

While every effort is made to keep prices low, it is sometimes necessary to increase prices at short notice. Wyndham Books reserve the right to show new retail prices on covers which may differ from those advertised in the text or elsewhere.

Postage and Packing Rate

UK: 22p for the first book, plus 10p per copy for each additional book ordered to a maximum charge of 82p. **BFPO and Eire:** 22p for the first book, plus 10p per copy for the next 6 books and thereafter 4p per book. **Overseas:** 30p for the first book and 10p per copy for each additional book.

These charges are subject to Post Office charge fluctuations.